Forever Remain

'Quizzing glass and quill, into my sedan chair and away —— the 1700s rock!'

WHEN NOT BUMPING ABOUT 18th century London in my sedan chair or exchanging gossip with perfumed and patched courtiers in the gilded drawing rooms of Versailles, I write award-winning Georgian historical romances and mysteries (with lashings of romance). My books are set in 1700s Georgian England, with occasional crossings to continental Europe. I pull up the reins at the French Revolution where I lost a previous life at the guillotine for my unpardonably hedonistic lifestyle as a layabout aristo!

lucindabrant.com
lucindabrant@gmail.com
facebook.com/lucindabrantbooks
twitter.com/lucindabrant
pinterest.com/lucindabrant
Sign up for Lucinda's newsletter at lucindabrant.com

ROXTON LETTERS VOLUME TWO
A COMPANION TO THE ROXTON FAMILY SAGA

Lucinda Brant

ISBN 978-1-925614-21-3

10 9 8 7 6 5 4 3 2 (i)

for

Lucinda's Gorgeous Georgian Gals

CONTENTS

DAIR DEVIL LETTERS

PROUD MARY LETTERS

SATYR'S SON LETTERS

LUCINDA BRANT BOOKS

— Alec Halsey Mysteries —

DEADLY ENGAGEMENT

DEADLY AFFAIR

DEADLY PERIL

ALEC HALSEY MYSTERIES: BOOKS 1–3

— Salt Hendon Books —

SALT BRIDE

SALT REDUX

SALT HENDON COLLECTION

—The Roxton Family Saga —

NOBLE SATYR

MIDNIGHT MARRIAGE

AUTUMN DUCHESS

DAIR DEVIL

PROUD MARY

SATYR'S SON

ETERNALLY YOURS

FOREVER REMAIN

FOREWORD

It is with great pleasure that His Grace and I offer this the second in the two-volume set of letters, being a selection of correspondence authored by my esteemed forebears, and persons important in their daily lives.

We were overjoyed with the reception the first volume received from academicians just over two years ago, and we hope this selection will be of equal interest, and provide further illumination into lives lived in the reign of His Majesty King George the Third.

The letters selected here are weighted heavily in favor of those pieces of correspondence that discuss family and family matters. For it is births, deaths, and marriages which occupy the Roxton extended family during the second half of the eighteenth century. And so it is to family my husband and I wish to focus, taking the reader on a journey into the domestic heart of the dukedom, when the sixth duke and his duchess were laying the foundation of a dynasty. This not only included the raising of eight children to adulthood, but also managing the wider family association of marriages and births that would consolidate their position, and those of their inner family circle, at the very apex of their class in their own time, and which has continued to have ramifications to this day, as we are on the cusp of entering a new century.

Readers seeking to gain insight into the political views of the various correspondents, hoping to read letters filled with the governmental machinations and manoeuvrings of members of both houses of Parliament, as well as to glean comments on political events, and the political climate in this kingdom and in far-off kingdoms, will be disappointed. As will those seeking insight into the religious and philosophical beliefs of family members. Such topics may be touched on briefly, and no doubt can be discerned from remarks made in passing in the letters selected here, but in general, any letters of a political or religious or fractious nature have been set aside as not fitting the purview of what we set out to achieve with this collection of correspondence. No apologies are made for these omissions.

By purposely selecting only those letters which concentrate on the day-to-day social interactions and domestic details of family members, the Duke and I wish the reader to gain a greater understanding of the true character and nature of the correspondents. For it is only through the expression of feelings and the revelation of our innermost thoughts that a person can truly be known.

It must be reiterated that this publication and its companion are published in a private capacity, and are not for public consumption. They are meant for the shelves of select persons with an academic interest in the Roxton lineage who wish to gain a deeper insight into their lives and motivations.

Again, His Grace and I wish to acknowledge the tireless efforts of the Treat Librarian, Sir Elliott Fortescue, Bt., and his assistant, Mr. Percival Mandrake, and also Professor Sir Marcus West-Hamilton, and the eminent French linguist Mr. Auguste Martin. Particular to this volume is the scholarship of the distinguished diplomat Sir Bipin Narendra Deb, who kindly translated His Grace of Kinross's letter written in Hindi to his natural daughter, Mrs. Charles Fitzstuart, both father and daughter being capable linguists in that language of the subcontinent. Without the dedication of these gentlemen, this volume of letters, like its companion, would not have seen the light of day.

This second volume is dedicated to our children: Henry, Christopher, Deborah, Evelyn, and Lisa-Antonia.

Alice-Victoria Hesham
Her Grace the Most Noble Duchess of Roxton
May, 1898

FROM THE EDITORS

THE LETTERS AND DIARY ENTRIES in this the second of the two volumes follows the same chronology as set out in the first volume. The volume opens with correspondence from the early 1770s, and with a letter thought lost to the pages of history and discovered by chance in the Roxton archive—one of the great discoveries of this publication, for it is thought to be the only surviving letter in the hand of the second Earl of Strathsay, grandson of King Charles the Second. The second chapter contains letters from Kate, Lady Paget, to the fifth Duke, written in the 1760s, of relevance because of Her Ladyship's unique friendship with that Duke, and her particular relationship to the Lady Mary Fitzstuart Cavendish Bryce's second husband, the influential wool and cloth merchant Sir Christopher Bryce. Amongst the letters offered in the third chapter are ones penned by the fifth Duke, writing as a parent to his second son when he knew he was dying and yet determined to leave behind words of wisdom and of love for this young man whom, it is evident from his correspondence, he loved immeasurably. These letters exemplify what Her Grace eloquently explains in her foreword, and which is worth repeating here: It is only through the expression of feelings and the revelation of our inner most thoughts that a person can truly be known.

Readers are to note that certain names, words, phrases, and

sentences have been suppressed in particular letters and are indicated thus [*suppressed*], on the instructions of Their Graces, for which they, and we, make no apologies.

All translations from the French were meticulously carried out by Mr. Auguste Martin, and the translation from the Hindi by Sir Bipin Narendra Deb, G.C.I.E. The editors are most grateful to Mr. Percival Mandrake for his tireless work in collation and transcription of the originals of various correspondence, in this volume and the first (an omission of thanks from that volume rectified here with sincere apologies).

Sir Elliot Fortescue Bt., C.B.E.
Professor Sir Marcus West-Hamilton, G.C.M.G., O.B.E.
June, 1898

Note
Throughout this volume, where necessary, [5th] and [6th] has been inserted before 'Duke of Roxton' to distinguish father from son, lest the reader be confused as to which title holder is being addressed.

DAIR DEVIL LETTERS

THE EARL OF STRATHSAY TO MAJOR LORD FITZSTUART

The Right Honorable Earl of Strathsay, Charles House, Barbados, to Major Lord Fitzstuart, 17th Light Dragoons c/o Sir John Becher, Hollybrook House, County Cork, Ireland

[Letter sent while the Major was stationed with his regiment in Ireland, then forwarded and received by him while on active duty in the American Colonies during the American Revolutionary War. It has gone into family anecdote that upon reading his father's letter, the Major set the pages alight with his cheroot and tossed them onto the campfire. This then is a copy of that same letter, discovered by Mr. Percival Mandrake while cataloguing the Roxton archives. It is quite a discovery, for this is the only letter known to exist in the hand of Theophilus Fitzstuart, the second Earl of Strathsay. A hand-written note (by another hand) on the obverse of the letter states that this letter is a copy sent by Lord Strathsay to the sixth Duke for safe keeping in the event his son Major Lord Fitzstuart did not receive the original.]

Charles House, Barbados
December 1774

Dear Major,

Alisdair, I trust this letter finds you well and enjoying life in the service of our king. As you have been made aware by others, because you have not bothered to read any of my correspondence, I was and am against your commission. I wrote my opposition to His Grace of Roxton (the fifth duke not the present holder of the title) in the strongest possible language. Though this was after I learned of the fact and you were already on your way to join your regiment in Ireland. And now I am informed that regiment is off to fight the traitorous rebels in the American Colonies. So let me wish you well, and I pray you stay out of harm's way and return alive from the venture and in one piece. You cannot blame me for thanking providence that I have a second son, and that Charles is of a staid nature and thus would never risk his neck in such a wantonly foolish gesture.

While I am all admiration for your willingness to fight for King and Country against the rebellious colonials who dared to take up arms against his most sovereign Majesty, you would have been better placed learning how to manage your inheritance, marrying early, and producing an heir to follow on after you. You know that were you to marry, I would hand over the estate to you, and not leave it in the present Duke of Roxton's hands to manage. That admirable young man is a worthy successor to his father. I would dare to say worthier, and he does not need the added burden of looking after my affairs in England, but he will do so because his mother is my niece, and because you are his closest cousin. He at least knows what is due his name, and is prepared to shoulder the great burden of responsibility a great name requires. I live in hope that one day you will do the same.

No doubt you scoff because your father lives thousands of miles away from his responsibilities. But may I remind you that it was not by choice that I came out here to the Caribbean, though I now remain here of my own free will. That I ended up on a sugar plantation far from England, I now put down to providence. And if you will give me five more minutes of your time to read on you will see that your father does indeed have a conscience.

I do not seek your forgiveness, though I would like it. And while Charles and Mary are more inclined to allow me some latitude with the passing of time, I know you will not. I cannot blame you. I did not treat you, your mother, your brother, and your dear sister at all well. And with distance and time to reflect on my past, I am willing to admit I was a poor parent and an even worse husband. The breakdown of my marriage was my fault almost entirely. And because my eyes have been open to it, and also my heart, I ask that you take good care of your mother, to not blame her for her coldness and lack of feeling where her children are concerned. I do not doubt her lack of affection is due to the nature of your conception. She endured the marital bed out of a sense of wifely and dynastic duty, not because [*suppressed*]. She made no effort to please me or be pleased, [*suppressed*] could not hide her horror [*suppressed*] found me repulsive. In my ignorance, shame and anger, I [*suppressed*] and [*suppressed*] but she [*suppressed*]. In short, it was a degrading experience for us both [*suppressed*] and I failed [*suppressed*] the defect in her was not something which she was capable of correcting. She will never be warm-hearted. She is devoid of [*suppressed*] and is a creature who finds that aspect of life repugnant, and unnecessary to her existence.

A more experienced man would have seen her nature for what it was before we married. But as a callow young man I mistook coldness for shyness, frigidness for ignorance. His Grace the fifth Duke of Roxton tried to warn me. I should have listened, for His Grace had a vast experience of women and no doubt he saw, as I did not, that Charlotte possessed a temperament unsuited to physical intimacy. But it was the very fact the Old Duke had a libertine past before he married my niece that I foolishly mistook his wise counsel for one who was dismissive of your mother because he himself did not find her physically appealing. What a stupid ass I was!

You must be wondering where I am taking this discussion, and why I am confiding such intimate details to you and focusing on my past sins. It is because of my present situation that I now realise I was never in love with your mother, nor do I think she was ever in love with me. We were both enamoured of the idea of being married, and independent, and no doubt this drew us together. She wished to escape a life as a dependant of her brother, and forever a spinster. I wished to be out from under my mother's malevolent and wanton selfishness. Neither of us was prepared for the intimacy marriage brings.

Does it surprise you to learn your father was just as ignorant as his bride on his wedding night? And therein was my first of many mistakes. I was determined to remain chaste all because I had a mother who was a [*suppressed*]. Had she been a man she would have been celebrated as a great rake. But being female, she will forever be known as a [*suppressed*]. She was very beautiful, all her portraits attest to this and thus it is small wonder she had a legion of men courting her from a young age. She lacked the moral fiber and judgment to resist their [*suppressed*] overtures. And once corrupted, she became the corruptor, and was not above seducing any young man who took her fancy, where and when she pleased, and without any thought given for the persons living under her roof, namely her son. Because I was disgusted by her behavior, I was determined to remain a monk until I married.

At least you are not as foolish as your father, for you are not a monk, are you? Nor have you been since your seventeenth summer, when you sowed your wild oats too close to home and got a servant's daughter pregnant. This is not the place to lecture you on your youthful folly. However it will surprise you to learn that I am pleased you begat an illegitimate son, because at least I know I have an heir whose seed is fertile, and so I can expect you to produce legitimate sons when you finally marry a female worthy of your noble blood. And with carnal experience, which I hope you continue to satisfy with women paid for their services, and not virginal servants who stupidly allow themselves to fall with child, you will gain further experience in matters of the bedchamber.

You, unlike me, will then not be able to use ignorance as an excuse for your lack of ability to satisfy your bride in bed.

Which brings me to what I wished to tell you. I am a much better man in every sense of the word since I came to live here in Barbados, a paradise on earth. The passage of time, and the distance from home, has given me perspective. I am not only older but much wiser. Which is why I can tell you with confidence that I have fallen in love and this for the first time in my life. I never thought I would find love, or that love would find me, and at the ripe old age of five-and-fifty, but it did. Why do I write and tell you this? I have also written to your sister and brother with this news. Because I will not be returning to England. I shall remain here, and be buried here when the time comes, along with my common-law wife. For that is what Monica Drax is to me—my wife and my love. Monica is the acknowledged daughter of a sugar merchant and his mulatto mistress, and she recently gave birth to our twins, Barnaby and Bernadette. No two children could be more perfect or more loved and I am besotted with them, as I am with her.

You might as well know, for no doubt you will discover this one way or the other, so should hear it from me, Monica is younger than your brother Charles. Yet at two-and-twenty she is old enough to know her own mind and her own heart. We live openly as husband and wife, and with her family's blessing. She is mistress of my house, and is treated by all as if she is indeed my wife. I wish I could bestow upon her the title, and while I cannot do so, my servants and friends give her the respect had she been my wife and refer to her as 'my lady', which is only fitting, and makes me happy.

I do not mean you or your mother any disrespect. But I am here, and you there, and we shall never meet again. So do not concern yourself. Monica and I will never set foot on English soil, nor will our children, if I have any say in the matter, and thus I do not see any harm in living the way that I wish it to live if I could make wishes come true. If that offends you, so be it.

I mean to bestow upon Monica and our offspring, of which I hope there will be many, the plantation here in Barbados, the slaves attached to the estate, and half the wealth from the sugar produced. The other half you are to divide up with your brother and sister.

Which brings me to tell you that I have written to my attorneys in London instructing them that upon your marriage, to revert to you all responsibilities and rights to my English estates, and the income that derives from them being held in trust by His Grace of Roxton. If I could give up my earl's coronet and ermine to you now, I would gladly do that too. So you see, the sooner you marry, the sooner you may have as much of your inheritance that is within my power to bestow upon you.

There is enough news in this letter to last you several years' worth of letters from me. I will not write again to you directly because I know you will not answer me, and so I will seek news about your welfare from other sources. I will not send you my love or best wishes because I know you do not want them. I shall, however, pray for you, and keep you in my thoughts. And I will sign my mark as your father because nothing can take away kinship however much you despise and hate me and wish you could disown your own father. Take care, my son.

Your father,
Theophilus Strathsay

ANTONIA, DUCHESS OF KINROSS, TO CHARLOTTE, COUNTESS OF STRATHSAY

Antonia, the Most Noble Duchess of Kinross, Crecy Hall, Treat via Alston, Hampshire, to the Right Honorable Charlotte, Countess of Strathsay, Fitzstuart Hall via Denham, Buckinghamshire.

Crecy Hall, Hampshire
July, 1777

Dear Aunt,

Charlotte, I trust this letter finds you in better health and frame of mind than you were at Easter. And if you are still feeling the lingering effects of whatever it was that was ailing you then, I assure you that this letter from me now will, if not cure you of all your ills, offer you some respite at least until the wedding.

Wedding? Whose wedding you ask. I shall tell you about it in a moment, but first I must tell you the rest, and how it came to be that there is to be a wedding. Do not ask me for every little particular because I cannot give them to you, and even if I did know, it was told to me in confidence, so you will have to trust me that all that matters is the outcome which is that your son Alisdair is to be married.

That is correct, Charlotte. Your eldest son Alisdair is to be married, and soon. And so there is to be a wedding, and at Treat.

Alisdair has found his match, and it is a meeting of souls as well as hearts. They are a couple in love. He truly is in love with her, and she with him, and I state this as fact. You must be happy for him and for them both. And even if you do not believe as I do in fate and true love and happily-ever-afters, you must and will be happy for your son.

Love aside (though that is what is most important to me in any union) your son's choice of bride is one that should be gratifying to you and perhaps even make you happy, because she is a very suitable choice socially.

Aurora Talbot is Edward, Lord Shrewsbury's granddaughter, and Monseigneur and I we were her godparents. She is the daughter of Edward's eldest son, who died, along with her mother, when she was an infant. Rory (as she prefers to be called) and her brother Harvel, Lord Grasby, were orphaned and brought up by Edward. Harvel is Edward's heir, and as it so happens, one of Alisdair's boon companions. They attended Harrow together. So you see, Rory has a most suitable lineage, and one that even you must think worthy of the heir to an earldom.

If you are wracking your brain wondering if Rory has been intro-duced to you, or present at functions which you attended, then the answer it is yes. You do know her, but perhaps, like most people, you took little notice because she rarely if ever put herself forward. She has been a guest at Treat a number of times, in her grandfa-ther's company, though she tends not to go out into society, much preferring to spend her time in the pursuit of cultivating the pineapple fruit. So you see, she is a most singular and fascinating young woman. I need not make comment on this but I will. Rory is beautiful or Alisdair he would not have looked twice at her, would he? She possesses a delicate, refined beauty, not unlike a piece of fine porcelain. But make no mistake, Charlotte, my goddaughter knows her own mind, has a sharp intellect, and is the sweetest, most loving girl. She loves your son unreservedly and is his greatest champion. So it is no wonder Alisdair he fell in love with her. To see them together is to see true love blossoming before my eyes.

My son he has given the union his blessing, which should also please you. And it is Roxton's blessing and mine that is all Alisdair cares about. He does not intend to seek his father's approval or permission (he needs neither), but will write to him out of courtesy informing him of the match.

You must not feel neglected that he did not write to you himself, but asked that I do so. Letters to his father and to his brother were all the sitting he could suffer for one afternoon, and so he asked that I write to you so that you would receive the news as soon as possible. He asks that you come to Treat for the wedding, which will be within the next few weeks. I think my son he intends to write to you, too. And he has also written to Mary. It is hoped she will bring Teddy with her, which would be a fitting occasion for your granddaughter to be introduced to her Roxton relatives.

Oh, and so that you have the time to recover from the shock between now and then, I am enceinte. You do not have to tell me that for a woman of my age, who has a son approaching his third decade, it is quite shocking indeed. I agree with you. But Jonathon he will have an heir, and that is all I care about. And it is done. So there is nothing for you to do but accept it, and be pleased for us.

Your loving niece,
Antonia Kinross

MR. RADCLIFFE PLUME, ESQ., TO MAJOR LORD FITZSTUART

Mr. Radcliffe Plume, Esq., Charles House, Barbados, to Major Lord Fitzstuart, Fitzstuart Hall, Buckinghamshire and c/o His Grace the Most Noble Duke of Roxton, Treat via Alston, Hampshire, England.

[A paper attached to the parchment reads: Received on the eve of Major Lord Fitzstuart's marriage, and set aside until his return from a month's honeymoon. Opened in the presence of His Grace of Roxton, and Her Grace of Kinross, end August, 1777.]

Charles House, Barbados
June 1777

My dear Major, Your Lordship,

It is my sad duty to inform you of the death of your father, Theophilus James Fitzstuart, Earl of Strathsay, who was a resident of Barbados for some seventeen years.

You do not know me, but I knew your father well. We were the majority shareholders of a Sugar Cooperative, supplying sugar home to England. I had weekly, sometimes daily, dealings with His Lordship, and his family and mine were close enough to exchange dinner invitations. I am a widower and my son is back in England with his family. I feel keenly your loss, for he spoke of Your Lordship and of your brother Mr. Charles Fitzstuart, and of your sister the Lady Mary Cavendish, often and with sentimentality.

His Lordship and his family perished when a surprisingly unseasonable hurricane of unimaginable strength and destructive force decimated the island. Thousands have died, and there is not a house left habitable. Only a wing of this, your father's substantial house, still stands, and is providing the only shelter for those left alive, and those come to provide them succour and comfort. All ships in the harbor and their crews are lost. Most life on the island, be it plant or animal, is no more. I cannot adequately describe to you what I am seeing with my own eyes—it is beyond the comprehension of man, and appears to be what I presume hell must resemble for those souls sent there for their sins.

I should also inform you that while your father's body was recovered, that of his common-law wife, Monica Drax, and their two children, Barnaby and Bernadette Fitzstuart-Drax, have yet to be found. We do not hold out any hope of them being alive, given it is now some weeks since the hurricane struck. We presume they, like so many hundreds, nay thousands, of others, were swept out to sea and drowned when the storm surge engulfed the island.

Let me tell Your Lordship how your father died because I am certain you have a natural curiosity to know. Lord Strathsay was discovered under the debris of what had been his study. It seems he managed to find shelter under his desk, but even that sturdy object was lifted up and away by the ferocious winds, and your father was tossed away with it. His neck was broken by the winds and his body impaled on the splintered remains of a bookcase. The surgeon assures me that death would have been almost instantaneous from the break to his neck, and thus he would have been unaware of any suffering and what occurred to his body thereafter.

As proof of your father's passing, I enclose the ring he always wore and which he proudly told us was given to his father by his father, His Majesty King Charles the Second, His Lordship's grandfather. It was removed from his body in the presence of ship's surgeon Lt. Col. Dr. Ian McBride of the H.M.S. Endurance.

As you can appreciate, in this hot climate, and to ensure there is no spread of miasma and disease, all bodies recovered were buried as swiftly as possible. And while many were placed in a common pit, I made certain your father was buried here at his house. A stone will be placed over the grave in due course, once the island returns to some sense of normality. Though when that will be, is anyone's guess, for it will be years, if not decades, before we see the same prosperity as we have enjoyed these past twenty years or more. I intend to remain here at Charles House, which has become the administrative heart of the effort to restore the island, and will except to hear from Your Lordship in due course as to what is to be done with your father's estate, of which there are a dozen slaves who managed to survive, and who have been put to work in cleaning up and rebuilding what we can.

I was appointed executor of your father's last will and testament, of which I believe he sent a copy to reside with his lawyers in London, another copy to His Grace the Duke of Roxton, his cousin, as well as the copy I have in my possession. It is then probable you have already been informed of its contents by his lawyer or His Grace, or both. But it falls upon me to inform Your Lordship that while your father left his estate here to his common-law wife and the children he had by her, if they cannot be found, this estate will become yours in due course. There are other particulars I would rather not delve into here, and of which you must also be aware from his will.

I would urge Your Lordship to send a representative of the legal fraternity with a member of your family who knew your father well, so that in the event you wish to carry out an exhumation to be satisfied it is indeed your father we buried, this can be done as expeditiously as possible. I realise you have much at stake, the inheritance of his titles and estate being of prime importance, and having all doubt eradicated and your mind put to rest is paramount. I assure you that your representatives will be treated with the utmost cordiality and respect, and all particulars discussed and settled in a most satisfactory manner.

Rest assured, there was nothing your father could have done that he did not do to try and secure his survival, the survival of his family, retainers, and slaves. And this was told me by one of his most devoted men, Old Clive, a slave who had been with him since he first arrived on the island, and who had his confidence and had earned his respect.

May I offer up my sincere condolences to you and your family for the loss you have suffered. Your father was an excellent gentleman whom I was honored to call friend.

I await Your Lordship's instructions, and remain…

Your most obedient servant,
Radcliffe Plume

JONATHON, DUKE OF KINROSS, TO THE HON. MRS. CHARLES FITZSTUART

Jonathon, the Most Noble Duke of Kinross, Leven Castle via Kinross, Fife, Scotland, to the Honorable Mrs. Charles Fitzstuart, 21 Rue du Peintre Lebrun, Versailles, France.

[*Translated from the Hindi.*]

Leven Castle, Fife
August, 1777

My darling mouse-deer, I think of you every day. I wonder how you fill your days. If you have made friends in your adoptive country. Does Charles give you enough of his time? Are you lonely? Is Mrs. S proving a help or a hindrance to a young girl just married? How are your language lessons progressing? Your *Baboo* Papa is full of questions. He misses your company, and your scolds. He has too much time on his hands and so his thoughts fill with worries. You must think him slipping into his dotage. For where was his worry when we lived on the subcontinent and your *Baboo* Papa went off for weeks at a time to the north, leaving you in the care of your ayah. There was one time, or was there two? when the floods made it impossible for me to return home to you for two months. Do you remember? I was not greatly worried then because you were with people I trusted with your life, and mine. And that separation I could endure, knowing we would be reunited. This separation is different, and feels vast and lonely and forever.

Forgive your *Baboo* Papa because he is being selfish. You are wise enough to know that my loneliness is compounded because I am living a life I do not relish or want, but feel obligated to live. And not only have I been parted from my only child, but separated from the love of my life, and this at the very beginning of our married life. We were up before the parson one day and the next I was on my way to this icy and most decidedly draughty place I am very sure has yet to be discovered by a cartographer.

It is the opposite to the subcontinent in temperature, out of the boiling vat to be plunged into an icy netherworld, and this the height of summer! Though I will grant that the landscape is breathtaking in its austerity and muted colors. The poverty of its people is astonishing, yet their resilience and pride are remarkable. For that alone I will do my best by them and remain to create something worthy, for them and their children. And I mean to bring my new duchess here in time, when the house is fit for her habitation. You know your *Baboo* Papa can sleep on a woven mat on hard ground as long as he can look up at the night sky. But my dearest wife shall have rooms befitting her rank. And I refuse to be outdone and outshone by her first duke! Therein lies the competition, and I have ever been competitive, have I not?

Sarah-Jane, let your *Baboo* Papa be serious for a moment and express his hope that in time you will be reconciled to my marriage, and to your stepmother, the new Duchess of Kinross. Surely you see now, or at the very least Charles, who is her closest cousin, has reassured you, that Antonia is a woman of deep feeling, and thus she does truly love me. I love her unreservedly, and with my whole heart. That should suffice for you to embrace her, and set your mind at ease. For what is age but a number?

You expressed your concern that I require a legal heir and that my wife is not of an age to be able to provide me with one, and this was enough of a reason for us not to marry. You may be right, in that now I am a duke, I am presumed to want an heir. But I am not needful of it. Nor do I believe that my wife incapable of giving me a child. We will have at least one. That is all there is to it. A love like ours demands it. But if it does not happen, then so be it. I am ever philosophical. Your *Baboo* Papa will leave the matter in Shiva's hands, and pray to his wife Parvati, for is she not the goddess of fertility, love, and devotion?

You do know that had it been in my power to legally make you my heir, I would have done so a thousand times over. You would have made a wonderful Duchess of Kinross. But I am of the opinion your husband would have found it difficult to reconcile his revolutionary principles and hold his head as high as he does amongst his colonial brethren, had he married the heir to a Scottish dukedom. His fellows would have scoffed at his ideals. That his father-in-law is a duke is hardly his fault, is it?

We are both destined to live forever with the consequences of my running off with your mother, a married woman. But I don't regret it. I cannot. She was never likely to be divorced from her husband, an abusive oaf, and I had to rescue her from him as soon as possible. To that end, and because we fell in love, we were prepared to spend the rest of our lives in sin. Fleeing to the subcontinent and a life there, where I knew I could make a life for us and the people would welcome us with open arms, was our only recourse. And it was not one either of us regretted. We looked to it with optimism, as a grand adventure. As long as we could be together, nothing else mattered. It never occurred to either of us that your mother would fall pregnant, and so quickly. Her marriage was barren. And did we care our child would be born out of wedlock? Did we think of the long term consequences for such a child? Of course not! We were in love, and we welcomed you into our lives and loved you with all our being. When your mother told me the news of her pregnancy I was so happy, we were so happy, to think we were to have a child together. All your mother ever wanted was to be a good wife and mother, and with me she was both. She loved you so very much. So you see, my darling dear, you are so loved and were so wanted and celebrated, that the disadvantage of your birth was and is a very minor detail.

I am needed elsewhere now, and as my time is not my own, and I must try and accomplish as much as I can before returning south, I will leave off now and write to you again very soon.

Your papa loves you and misses you, and sends you a thousand kisses.

Give my regards to Charles. I will reply to his letter in the next day or two and answer all his questions.

K

You see how self-important I have become. Now your *Baboo* Papa is a duke, he signs with a flourish and only with his initial. xo

*Major Lord Fitzstuart, H.M.S. Reliant, Barbados, to Lady Fitzstuart,
Fitzstuart Hall, Buckinghamshire, England.*

H.M.S. Reliant
September, 1777

My dearest darling wife,

Wife! The best word in the world. For you are the best thing that
has ever happened to me, my dearest darling Delight. Forgive me
if this letter drips sentiment, but when I take the time to be still,
to sit and think, or when I am in my bunk falling asleep to the
motion of the waves, my thoughts are all of you. I think of our
time on Swan Island and wish I were back there with you. I think
of the future we will have together when I return. I even dare to
imagine our children and what they will look like. Ha! I do have
too much time on my hands, don't I?

I started this letter then put it aside. I may do this several times
before it is done. I know you will forgive me if it is not the master-
piece it should be. In truth it may be the longest piece of writing I
have ever undertaken, and that includes any reports I sent your

grandfather over the years detailing my activities. I always preferred to speak with our Spymaster General in person.

Delight, know that your dearest husband (the second best word in the world) is in his customary robust health. So is his batman. Mr. Farrier sends his regards, and says to assure Her Ladyship that he is keeping His Lordship out of trouble as best he can. But what trouble can I get myself in confined to a ship out in the Atlantic? You may well ask! But I am glad I have Farrier with me and I know you are, too.

I am not idle. I spend my days 'learning the ropes', to be a sailor! I can now 'work the ropes' and tie all manner of knots. The men were at first wary of my inquisitiveness and my willingness to work alongside them. For what gentleman, and most definitely not a nobleman, stands shoulder to shoulder with the common sailor. The officers tried to dissuade me from fraternizing, but as the captain sees no harm in it he does not stop me. And his men are happy to have me, for I amuse them with my questions. Captain Willis also knows I'd rather throw myself overboard than be confined to a cabin playing at chess, reading, or writing letters home (except to you, Delight), which is what gentile passengers are supposed to do while aboard. They also avoid the sea air and the blistering heat. I'm having none of that, and as far as I am concerned, it is better to be out on deck smelling the salt air and turning brown than being stuck in cramped quarters, pacing back and forth and breathing the smoke from my cheroot!

Which reminds me to warn you that when next you see me you will find my hands calloused and my arms and face a nice shade of nut brown. But you will be pleased that I am cultivating a pirate beard, just for you. It is coming along nicely despite Mr. Farrier's disapproval and objections to it. He sharpens my razor daily in expectation of me coming to my senses before we make land, and before I return to you. Pirate Dair won't fail you!

I have just had the most bracing, nay, breath-stopping adventure! And I survived to tell the tale, so you must not worry needlessly, Delight. Though I know you would never deny me a little amusement to counter the boredom of long days at sea. So let me tell you about it.

It was as thrilling as the heart-pounding anticipation of charging at full gallop at the enemy. That much I can say without hesitation. And it was just as satisfactory because it took me several attempts, and I had to muster all my courage. But I finally managed to climb all the way up to the topsail yard! What's that you ask? A yard is the cross beam of a mast to which the sails are lashed, and the topsail yard is the second sail, not the first, high above the deck, so your dear husband was extra courageous to go one better than the one he was dared to reach.

And once I had climbed to such dizzying heights, I ventured to inch myself along the rigging to sit halfway across, and there admire the view, which is afforded only to sailors and seagulls! The ocean stretches on endlessly to the horizon, the aspect only broken by the occasion wave. Though I did manage to catch sight of a mermaid! Or so I thought when her tail flicked up out of the water into the air. But I believe what I truly glimpsed was a different sea creature entirely. Most probably a whale. And when I chanced to glance below me, I discovered a crowd of upturned grinning faces. Every sailor who was not at his post had gathered to watch my attempt, no doubt in anticipation of my failure or falling to my death! And when I dared to get to my bare feet and stand tall, holding on and swaying with the ropes, I made my audience a sweeping bow as best I could from such a precarious position. A rousing cheer went up in response, to which I laughed and made a second bow. You would have enjoyed my performance, Delight. That was not the end of my escapade, for when I was once more safely on deck several of the men so far forgot themselves as to consider me one of their own, and they rushed forward, hoisted me up high and to more rousing cheers. Our carousing would have continued had not their master come to break up the revels and order his men back to their chores.

But please, my darling, do not fear I was in harm's way or that I was cavalier with my mortality. My life is now bound to yours, so I would never attempt anything that put my life in jeopardy. My honor on it. I love you too much to ever risk life and limb again. You are now what I live for, and you, and returning to you, are all I think about.

I will admit I was dared to do it. I said so earlier. But know that I would never have attempted the adventure had I not been confident of the outcome. I waited for a day when the seas were calm, so the ship was not rolling, which made the climb so much the easier. And you know I am an expert climber of trees, and my superior strength stood me in good stead for I was able to shimmy up the mast and along the ropes with surprising ease. I may be twice the width of these sailors who scurry all over the ship as monkeys do up a tree, but I am just as agile and more powerful in my wrists than they. Still, I am all admiration for their ability to go up and down the masts and along the topsails sorting the rigging and the sails and acting as lookouts, for it is a hazardous occupation and not for the faint of heart.

We have made land. It is five days since I last took up my quill and I am glad I wrote you of happier, more carefree times aboard ship, because I cannot do that now. We have dropped anchor in the harbor in what can only be described as hell on earth. I am assured by those who have been here before that Barbados was a paradise. No such place exists now. There are no people, no buildings, no vegetation, only destruction and wasteland. It is beyond my descriptive powers to do justice to the devastation and the suffering caused by the hurricane that visited this island. The winds were so severe trees have been stripped of their bark. The armory is no more. Stone buildings are reduced to rubble. A twelve-pound gun was carried a distance of 140 yards by the surge of the sea. It will take many years, if ever, before this place is habitable again.

It must have been a terrifying experience for all concerned, and my thoughts turn to my father and his young family. What torments and terror must he and they have suffered before their deaths? And not only he and his children, but all the poor souls living on this island? We are told that thousands lost their lives, and many more thousands on the surrounding islands. The British and French fleets are decimated. No fort, no house, nothing was left standing. Forgive me if I am repeating myself, but the carnage is beyond belief, and this from your husband who has been on a battlefield and witnessed carnage first hand.

I am back aboard ship to eat and sleep, and to write you the rest of this letter so I may send it on one of two ships which survived on the edge of the storm and which came into harbor to offer assistance, and now return to England for supplies, and with correspondence. I return to land tomorrow morning, and again to what is left of my father's house, for the official exhumation of his body. God knows what condition it is in, or if I will be able to stomach peering at it, but I have the ship's surgeon with me, to whom I can relay the information given me by Cousin Duchess of the healed fracture to my father's left arm. Mr. Plume, who I have found to be a fine fellow and very direct, has also offered his own recollections, for he remembers my father having several teeth drawn over the years.

As you can imagine, I just want the ghastly business over with so I can get on with my life. But I realize how necessary this is for my inheritance and our future, for while there is a scintilla of doubt as to whether my father is alive or dead, I cannot claim my birthright with confidence.

We discussed this before my departure, and I will remain true to my word to do all I can to find my father's children, dead or alive. Mr. Plume, and several of my father's slaves, are adamant that they could not have survived, but until their bodies are recovered how can we know this for certain? Mayhap we will never know. But if they are found alive, I will offer them safe passage to England, ensure they receive their inheritance, and see them settled as befits my father's love and care for them. If their bodies are recovered I will have them given a proper burial and beside my father's grave. It is the least I can do. As for the men he owned, I hate the very idea of human enslavement, as you know, and so they shall have their freedom and what compensation I can offer them to begin their lives anew. I know these are also your sentiments, and

Charles and Mary both agreed, though I would have done it anyway.

Mr. Farrier says I must rest, and he is right. And so I am signing off and sealing this letter with a kiss, and all my love. I cannot wait to return home to the comfort and warmth to be found in your arms. Do not think me selfish for not asking how goes the alterations to the hall, or how you are adjusting to life as its mistress, or if my mother has made herself agreeable if not pleasant. She will remain objectionable to the last about her move to the Dower House, and that has nothing to do with you and everything to do with the sort of woman she is. I have every faith in you handling her with the diplomatic dexterity you no doubt inherited from your grandfather.

I think of little else but you and our life at the hall, and it is a comfort to know you are there, safe, and waiting for me, and for me to know I have in you a helpmate whose sweet-natured serenity means you are able to deal with all manner of domestic crises (even my intractable parent). And I know you are bearing it all because you love me, and for that I love you all the more.

Love and kisses,
Dair with the pirate beard.

THE DUKE OF KINROSS TO HIS DUCHESS

Jonathon, the Most Noble Duke of Kinross, Flat 6, Forrester's Wynd, Lawnmarket, High Street, Edinburgh, Scotland, to Antonia, the Most Noble Duchess of Kinross, Crecy Hall via Alston, Hampshire.

Flat 6, Forrester's Wynd, Lawnmarket, High Street, Edinburgh
September, 1777

My heart's desire—Sweetheart,

I read your letter three times. I have it here beside me, open, and have read it yet again. My hand is shaking and my heart and head are pounding. My limbs have turned to syllabub.

I had just stepped out of a chair at the base of the stairs up to my lodgings here in the capital when a messenger handed me your letter. I was with a group of ruddy-faced gents, who had come to discuss debts and creditors and the future. All are in some way connected to my consequence—lawyers, kinsmen, a banker, my steward, two masters from neighboring lands, who spend more time here in Edinburgh than they do at their estates. I have settled my great uncle's debts to the great satisfaction of all, and am the hero of the hour. The point is, this hero was surrounded by a group of sturdy men, and they no taller than my shoulder, when your husband was unmanned by your news and was on the verge of collapse. My knees gave way and I lunged for the closest fellow's shoulder and used it as a crutch to stop myself from planting my face on the flagging. I am sure they thought I had suffered a heart seizure from the climb, for this place is very steep and there are stairs everywhere.

I felt the greatest fool to react to your news the way I did, and yet I did not care because you have made me the happiest of men, and not only me. When the crowd around me learned the news, the cheer that went up almost deafened me, and only added to my discomfort. And now I am grinning like a fool because I did not think it possible to feel happier than I did on our wedding day when I slipped a wedding band on your finger and made you mine.

Did I not tell you we would have a child, sweetheart? My prayers to Parvati have been answered! Do I feel for your position when you tell me you are sick every morning and now cannot stand the smell or taste of your favorite beverage? Of course I do! But it does not wipe the grin off my face. Nothing can. I walk about as if on a cloud, and everyone I pass possibly thinks me soft in the head. I do not care.

One thing is certain. I am coming home to you as soon as possible. What is most important is that I am with you, not hundreds of miles away. My steward, lawyer, banker, and anyone who matters to the estate agrees with me. The significance of your pregnancy to these people, and to my estate and the people who rely on me now I am their laird and duke, cannot be stressed enough. My elevation to the dukedom gave them hope, but your news gives them a future.

So I shall be home as quickly as it is possible for me to be so. Swift horses and good weather should see me returned to your arms by the end of the month. And then you may berate me to your heart's content for the condition you now find yourself in, and as you say at your age. Ha! Age! That is of no consequence to either of us, remember? May you never use that as an excuse with me again for though I am sure you castigate yourself every morning that what got you into this predicament was falling in love with a man who finds you utterly desirable and would, if it were in his power to do so, make love to you ten times a day.

Mayhap you are embarrassed to be pregnant at what you deem 'your age'? Did you feel so when you were pregnant with your sons? Of course you did not! Why would you? And I am very sure Monseigneur strutted about like a prize Dartmouth cock when you told him the news he was to be a father, and he in his middle years. So I give you fair warning, that this husband of yours intends to strut, and just as hard and as proud as he did. I have already started! For when I was enthusiastically congratulated by my kinsmen come with me from Fife, I know my chest swelled and I grinned. I did. I am sure my chest expanded even more when these men expressed their delight and excitement to think that their new duke has had the title for less than a year and already he is married, and will provide the dukedom with an heir in the new year. So my chest-puffing and strutting is justifiable.

I should tell you something of my stay in Scotland's capital, a more hilly up and down place as ever I have visited. The castle on its crag looms large over the landscape, and is not unlike a boil on a green giant's buttock, sticking up and out and looking painful, when everything around it is pleasant and green and damp. But for all that, it is a majestic sight, one that warms the Scottish blood in my veins.

I cannot fault the hard-faced locals who go about their business with solemn circumspection and purpose. Their townhouses are very tall and some six to eight stories in height, with several families living to a floor. There being no social distinction in the districts, for poor and rich live in close proximity, often in the same lodgings, it is only in the number of rooms and on which level a family chooses to reside which provide the clue as to the status of the occupants. The middle and higher floor levels are occupied by the wealthy and those with status, and the lower floors are crammed with the poor. Which is in direct contrast to what occurs in London, is it not, where the servants occupy the garrets. Not so here. There is talk and plans have been submitted for a planned city to be built on the other side of the loch that divides the castle and the surrounding areas from the rest of the lowlands. If it does go ahead, I shall buy into it, for I want my duchess and our child to live in a suitably comfortable and grand establishment. Besides, the merchant in me tells me it will be an excellent investment.

Many wealthy merchants, and those with title, live outside the walls of the city in houses befitting their rank. And it is only when you travel farther across the forth into Fife and beyond that you encounter estates that equate to the English equivalent of a grand mansion set in parkland. I am told that one such estate has a hot house for growing exotic fruits, and that the lord had built for his lady a large structure that resembles the pineapple. I would dearly love to see such a sight, and perhaps when you return here with me next summer, we can search out this pineapple for ourselves. I may start making enquiries and have my steward write to His Lordship with a request for a visit. Your goddaughter Rory will be most envious were we to visit this stone replica of her most favored fruit.

I realize this small excursion into my surroundings is most unsatisfactory for one such as you who has an unquenchable thirst for knowledge, but I must most reluctantly sign off this letter and have it sent at once, so that you will receive it as soon as possible. I have a few days of meetings in the capital to settle my affairs here in the north until my return in the spring. It is as well I have complete faith in my steward, a gentleman aptly named Mr. Colin Record. Between he and Ffolkes—to whom I have given my proxy and who will remain to catalog the library to his satisfaction—I have every confidence the repairs and renovation to the estate will continue on apace in my absence.

I count the hours until I am in your arms and we can once again indulge ourselves in [*suppressed*]. [*suppressed*] misses you and lets me know each morning. Does [*suppressed*] as much as [*suppressed*] for you? God this wanting makes me feel as if I am fifteen again in need of [*suppressed*] and that's all your fault, you wicked woman. Has a man ever desired a woman as much as I desire you? I shall [*suppressed*] and [*suppressed*] and you will [*suppressed*].

Your strutting rooster,
K

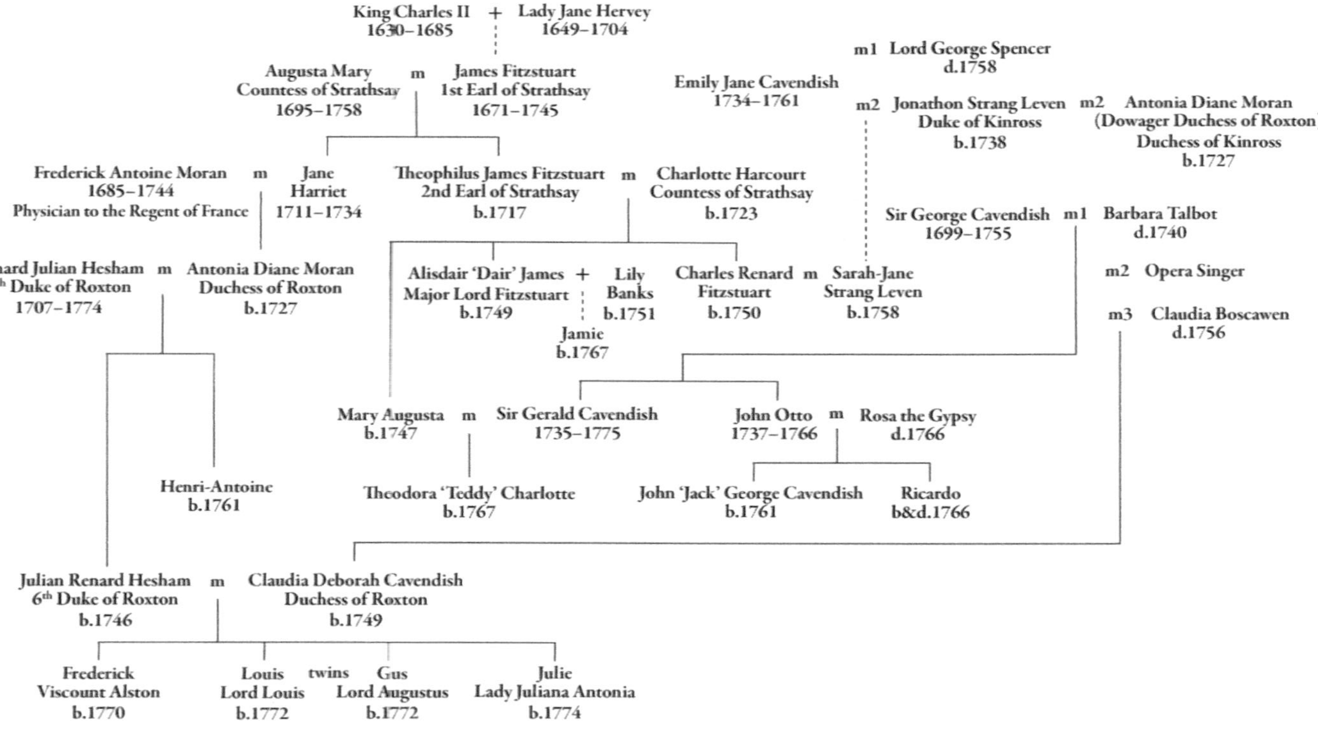

King Charles II 1630–1685 + Lady Jane Hervey 1649–1704
Augusta Mary Countess of Strathsay 1695–1758 m James Fitzstuart 1st Earl of Strathsay 1671–1745
Emily Jane Cavendish 1734–1761
m1 Lord George Spencer d.1758
m2 Jonathon Strang Leven Duke of Kinross b.1738
m2 Antonia Diane Moran (Dowager Duchess of Roxton) Duchess of Kinross b.1727
Frederick Antoine Moran 1685–1744 Physician to the Regent of France m Jane Harriet 1711–1734
Theophilus James Fitzstuart 2nd Earl of Strathsay b.1717 m Charlotte Harcourt Countess of Strathsay b.1723
Sir George Cavendish 1699–1755 m1 Barbara Talbot d.1740
m2 Opera Singer
m3 Claudia Boscawen d.1756
Renard Julian Hesham 5th Duke of Roxton 1707–1774 m Antonia Diane Moran Duchess of Roxton b.1727
Alisdair 'Dair' James Major Lord Fitzstuart b.1749 + Lily Banks b.1751
Charles Renard Fitzstuart b.1750 m Sarah-Jane Strang Leven b.1758
Jamie b.1767
Mary Augusta b.1747 m Sir Gerald Cavendish 1735–1775
John Otto 1737–1766 m Rosa the Gypsy d.1766
Henri-Antoine b.1761
Theodora 'Teddy' Charlotte b.1767
John 'Jack' George Cavendish b.1761
Ricardo b&d.1766
Julian Renard Hesham 6th Duke of Roxton b.1746 m Claudia Deborah Cavendish Duchess of Roxton b.1749
Frederick Viscount Alston b.1770
Louis Lord Louis b.1772 twins Gus Lord Augustus b.1772
Julie Lady Juliana Antonia b.1774

PROUD MARY LETTERS

KATE, LADY PAGET, TO THE [FIFTH] DUKE OF ROXTON

Kate, Lady Paget, Casa Rosa, vicino Ponte di Marmo via Borra, Quartieri Veneziato, Livorno, to His Grace the Most Noble [5th] Duke of Roxton, the White House, Third Hill Residences, Constantinople.

Casa Rosa, vicino al ponte di marmo di via Borra, Quartieri
Veneziano, Livorno
August, 1767

My dear Roxton,

You requested in your most recent letter for me to tell you something about Livorno. I was most surprised that you have never visited here, that you did not pass through this port on your way to Rome. But then I remembered you said you travelled overland from Paris so that you could visit Milan, Modena, and Florence before going on to Rome, and that you had a specific reason for visiting Modena. Although, Antonia did confide in me in her letter that the physician you consulted there about your little son's condition was unable to provide you with any answers, and even less hope!

I pray that having settled in a house in Constantinople, you are now at leisure to consult far and wide the physicians of Islam, and who you are hopeful have more knowledge about the falling sickness and its treatment than our physicians here in the west. Perhaps the change of environment and diet will offer your little boy some respite from his seizures?

And before I forget (yet again) and give you an account of this, my adopted city, I wish to send my love to you and Antonia on being reunited with your eldest son and heir. How many years have passed since you were all together as a family? Julian must be much changed, and I do not mean in appearance only. From what you told me of the reports from his godfather, he has grown into a worthy young gentleman of whom you are justifiably very proud. I do not need to remind you I understand completely your anxiousness at this reunion, and for it to go beyond your expectations, particularly for Antonia's sake. And I do hope you will write me an account of that most auspicious of occasions so that I may rest easy knowing the mother of your son has been reunited with her child to the mutual satisfaction of all parties.

I have strayed again from my purpose, have I not? So here is my précis of Leghorn (as we English call it, though I do my best to refer to it as the local people do and that is Livorno).

A great mixture of races resides here within this fortress town— Moors, Arabians, Turks, and all sort of Europeans, which I suppose is to be expected in a port where ships dock from many parts of the Mediterranean and beyond. These ships sail in as close as they can, this being a shallow water port, and then their goods are off-loaded onto smaller boats to be brought to shore. Once on dry land, they are sorted at the docks and then taken to enormous warehouses for further sorting. Those officials who supervise are not there to collect customs, as this sovereign state is free of such duties, and thus they spend their time keeping the peace and ensuring the smooth operation of the transfer of goods, and that none are stolen.

There is all manner of cargo, from grain to tobacco, sugar, and what may surprise you (it did me), an over abundance of dried cod and herring. Why you ask? It is for the local population and those beyond the walls for their Friday meal, when the papists are forbidden to partake of meat and dairy products of any kind, and also for the eves of feasts days. My housekeeper tells me that what with all the religious festivities, when Fridays and Saturdays and Lent days are added up together, Catholics spend over a third of the year without meat, eggs, butter, cheese, and lard! Imagine going without a good egg in the morning, or milk in one's tea or coffee? You certainly would not abide such dictates, and I dare say, were you a papist, would thumb your nose at the cardinals and Inquisition, and if I know you, get away with it, too. Damn you!

And yet, for all its papist dictates and sinister figures of the Inquisition skulking in shadows, hoping to pounce on those who dare to go against the teachings of the Church and eat meat on a Friday, this town is remarkably tolerant of other faiths. But that is an expedience of its wise rulers. The Medici, despite their ennoblement, were first and foremost bankers and merchants, and thus ever pragmatic. Where there is great commerce, coin takes precedence over God.

Christians, both Catholic and Protestant, Jews, and Islamists are able to worship freely here, and without fear. There are synagogues, and temples, and even an English cemetery!

So if I were to die here tomorrow, I could safely be buried in consecrated Protestant earth. I am told it is the only English cemetery in all of the Italian states. It is fenced and well tended, and many wealthy merchants have been laid to rest under impressive monuments.

With an English cemetery, one would then expect there to be a large community of our nationals living here. But that is not the case. It is a small community of only a few dozen families. But they are very visible economically, and given our mercantile preeminence, are exceedingly vocal about their wants and needs. The British factory (as these English merchants banded together are known) are well organized into a mercantile corporation, and do very well for themselves.

Of course, they are merchants born and bred and I will tell you how starved they are for good society: when it was known that I, the widow of a much-decorated admiral lord, had taken up residence here, it was as if the Queen herself had come amongst them! You chuckle and shake your head, but it is so. I have not had dinner at home in over a month, and while it is all very well to be feted and scraped to, I would prefer in my time of life to have a quieter existence, particularly with my failing sight not allowing me to gauge the mood of the room as well as I would like.

How I miss catching your eye from across a crowded drawing room and sharing a raised brow at some creature's outlandish outfit or a dandy's appalling wig looking more poodle than hair, and you pulling that face which would have me ducking behind my fan to hide my smile. But most of all I miss that dead stare, the one where I am convinced you can look straight through persons who bore you, so that they become as a ghost and might as well not be there at all, much you care for their conversation or their groveling addresses.

Come to think on it, you would not like Livorno at all. While you might approve of the townhouses on the canals along the via Borra where I have my apartment, which are uniform and spacious and there is a hint of Venice about the aspect, the company which I keep would not suit. Perhaps if you were to visit incognito, leaving your ducal coronet at the fortress wall. Visiting as His Grace of Roxton would fatigue you. Besides, this town is not large enough for the two of us! Ha!

[Paragraph of four or five sentences unreadable.]

I should have started a fresh page, or perhaps another letter, and sent what I had already written, but I could not or you may have surmised something untoward had happened to me to end so abruptly such a mundane correspondence.

Oh, my dearest friend! I have the most wonderful, wonderful news to impart. My son—and he has given me permission to call him that in private, though he will call me Kate while his adoptive parents live—has left Lucca and is here with me now. Yes! Christopher is here in my apartment. In truth it has been two weeks since I began my letter to you, for he walked through my door while I was here at my desk, and I was so shocked to see him that I spilled ink and forgot my letter altogether. I know you will forgive me.

Christopher and I have spent every waking moment since his arrival talking, and he talking of a future which includes me... Renard, I cannot convey to you the euphoria I am feeling except to equate it with the very same feeling I had when I first held him in my arms as a newborn. The feeling is that powerful, that overwhelming, that even now, as I ink this news to you, tears are filling my eyes, so that if my eyesight was poor before, it is even worse as I write this all down! So please do forgive this old lady her handwriting and the splotches to the page.

Did you ever expect such an outcome? I know you hoped, as I did, that my boy would come to his senses and see that all I ever wanted was to be a small part of his life. When I wrote to you of my first and only meeting with him late last year, he was still part of the De Nobili triangle. I was convinced he intended to continue in his vocation as a cicisbeo and would forevermore be known as Cristoforo.

What altered to make him change, you ask, when he has been the contractual gentleman companion and lover of other men's wives for a decade? And this last contract has been to the wife of a politically powerful Lucchesi count, Maddalena De Nobili, who was so taken with him as her companion-lover that she wanted, nay begged, him to sign a second contract for another two years, and her husband added his voice to hers!

I will never fathom how these arrangements are conducted so civilly, with legally-binding contracts, and all parties concerned, most particularly the husband and the wider community, accepting this 'love triangle' as if it is an everyday occurrence. No one looks down their nose on the cicisbeo, and everyone sees it as an honor and a stepping stone to greater things. The young gentlemen of the Italian aristocracy scramble about to acquire such a position, and I am told that as Christopher has been accepted as one of them, indeed, much sought after, is a great honor indeed.

You roll your eyes at me when I tell you I do not approve of my son as part of such a marital ménage a trois. And no, I am not being prudish, and well you know it! After all, you may well say he is following in my salacious footsteps, at the very least, his birth father's. Sir George was no saint, in and out of the bedchamber. But what I am referring to is Christopher's many and varied tasks out of the bedchamber as cicisbeo to a married woman. It is the servile nature of such a position, of him being at her beck and call, and the husband not only tolerating it, but being part of it all! You would never have bowed to such an arrangement. Jump into bed with a married woman, yes, but take her husband's place at the theatre and on outings and the like, and be obliged to fetch and carry her fan? Absolutely not! Your arrogance would never have allowed you to be anyone's lap dog.

I should not cast aspersions on an arrangement that is as foreign to me as Catholicism and the food (though I do enjoy the food!). After all, it is not my country, and it is not my social circle. But he is my son and an Englishman born and bred, and I would much prefer he spend his time as a muddy-booted squire, than as a silk-clad, perfumed jackanapes to a painted Italian countess.

No! I have not been in my cups to wish my son returned to the backwaters of the Cotswolds where he grew up, when all I ever did when he was a child was bemoan such a provincial upbringing. Laugh all you like! What I most wished for has certainly come to pass, for ten years living amongst the Tuscan nobility has transformed him into a most polished and accomplished gentleman. He does not walk, he glides. He does not merely move, he slithers. He does not talk, he converses, and in three languages, if it is required. He dances like a master, can fence to save his life, strums a mandora and plays the viola, and would be your equal for sartorial elegance. And if all these things are a measure of his assiduousness as a student of cicisbeism, and complete transformation, one can extrapolate this into the bedroom and confidently assume that he is a consummate lover, and like you, well able to satisfy his lovers in every particular.

Am I jealous you ask? Why yes! I most certainly am! To think he gives of his time and his talents to these women, and with the husband's permission, while I was never permitted to even be known to him as his aunt while he was growing up because I might infect him with my licentiousness, sticks in my throat like a fishbone. But I can hear you say that I now have had the last laugh, given my illegitimate son, brought up as a squire's son has transformed from backwater grub to aristocratic butterfly! So it must be in the blood, and no amount of hayracking and cider was going to make an ounce of difference. I have won, have I not?

It is a hollow victory because I do not, despite their disdain of me, wish my sister and her husband ill. But I would be lying to you and myself if I did not tell you when Christopher told me he had received a letter from his adoptive father that my sister, his 'mother,' was ill, I was not as upset as I should have been. I did try to appear so for his sake.

I do not wish for my sister to be ill, and I am exceedingly grateful to her and my dull brother-in-law for raising Christopher as their own, but it was news of her illness which provided the catalyst for his decision to give up this way of life he has here in Tuscany. Indeed, he has decided to quit Italy altogether and return to England to be with her.

And am I jealous that it took my sister's illness for him to come to his senses? Why, of course I am. But I do not let on to him, for he would not understand my resentment. And I would not want to jeopardize the delicate balance to our reconciliation. And so I bite my tongue and nod and agree and enter into all his plans. I can hear in his voice the love he has for Sophie, that she is in truth his mother, though I was the one who carried him in my womb, and went through the pain of childbirth to give him life.

And whatever the animosity between him and his 'parents' for their deception at not telling him the truth of his birth, which led him to run away to the Continent, he loves her, and he loves his father, and forgives them. And I know that none of my letters of entreaty, and the fact I settled here to be closer to him held any sway with his decision-making. And I must live with this and accept it, and be thankful that I am permitted a small piece of him.

I had Fran make me a coffee, and I went up to the turret that gives a splendid view of the harbor, to clear my thoughts, and because Christopher wished to speak to me of the future. Now I have returned, with my thoughts clearer, and wish to ask your forgiveness for a letter that started one way and has ended in quite another direction.

I will write again soon and let you know my plans, and what the future holds for me and my son. Ah! To be able to write those two words makes my heart sing.

Give my love to Antonia, and tell her I am thinking of her with her two sons, particularly more so now that I am able to be a mother again. Enjoy your sojourn amongst the Ottomans. You asked in your previous letter if I would care for you to bring me a little something back to England. I would, thank you. Let it be a silk turban and perhaps one of those shawls, so that I can look the part of a respectable matron, though I can assure you I never shall be!

Until next time, dearest friend,
All my love,
Kate

KATE, LADY PAGET, TO THE [FIFTH] DUKE OF ROXTON

Kate, Lady Paget, Casa Rosa, vicino Ponte di Marmo via Borra, Quartieri Veneziato, Livorno, to His Grace the Most Noble [5th] Duke of Roxton, the White House, Third Hill Residences, Constantinople.

Casa Rosa, vicino al ponte di marmo di via Borra, Quartieri
Veneziano, Livorno
August, 1767

My dear Roxton,

Your letter arrived the day after mine was sent, and so I am replying immediately so you know I received it, and because I must relate an incident that occurred, which, if I do not ink it now, I shall not want to write about it at all. But I must tell you, not only because you will find it amusing, but because you are well acquainted with the main actors in this tragic comedy. Naturally, you may share this with Antonia (I know you will anyway, but for what it is worth, she has my permission to read it).

Christopher has decided to return to England. I know I told you so in my previous letter, and my disappointment in us not having time spent alone together. But the good news is I shall follow, not immediately, but within six months. I may have to settle in Bath until such time as I can move closer. This depends on my sister and her husband, and how they take the news that their son is determined that I shall be part of his life, and thus their lives. How we will manage it all, I know not. But he does. And I suppose, given he managed to live a life within a triangle of husband, wife, and lover, he can adapt that to a life within a triangle of adoptive parents, birth mother, and their shared son!

My life, if nothing else, is interesting.

So this incident. It happened late last night. If it had involved anyone else but Christopher, I would have found more in it to amuse me. When it happened I was shocked, and every inch a mother. This morning, upon reflection, I found the humor in it and almost spilled my coffee when I burst into spontaneous laughter, with the image of the previous night's escapade popping into my mind's eye. Christopher is unscathed, and dear boy that he is, he was far more concerned about the episode's effect on me, than any injury done the Fittleworths' pride, or his modesty!

Oh dear. I have just spent five minutes wiping away tears of laughter because the more I thought about it, and what you would say or do had you been in a similar situation, the more I found to amuse myself. Of course you will raise that eyebrow of yours, and the corner of your mouth, too, and say that you would never have got yourself in such a situation in the first place, but I digress… Let me tell you a little of the background to events.

In my euphoria at having Christopher walk back into my life, all other considerations, appointments, etc. and so forth, slipped my mind. It is well I have a housekeeper who is beyond price, she is also the most marvelous cook, and her husband acts as my major domo. They are coming with us to England. I cannot live without them, or Fran, and they, mercifully, have agreed to leave behind their homeland to take care of me.

Again I digress. So while my housekeeper remembered I was having guests to stay, I did not. So here was I, sitting down to breakfast with Christopher, and in the turret, with its views of the harbor, and a lovely cooling breeze, watching a magnificent sloop flying the flag of the Dutch Netherlands drop anchor, when I am informed that Lord and Lady Fittleworth have arrived.

Good God! I'd forgotten all about Fanny and Fred coming to stay. Of course, at the time we had corresponded I had welcomed their visit. Fred is here in his official capacity as English consul to the Florentine court, to meet with the British Factory. A number of merchants have raised concerns on some trade and legal issues I cannot remember, and would not bore you with even if I did.

And as I have stayed with them in Florence on numerous occasions and enjoyed their hospitality enormously, I could not say no. Though, had I known Christopher would be living with me, I would not have hesitated in the least to put them off, or to have found them a townhouse of their own (though these are scarce to rent in this quarter).

As you are well aware, Fanny Fittleworth is not to be trusted with any man to whom she takes a fancy. She strays often, and he is a jealous husband, which is tiresome. It's not as if their marriage was a love match! Far from it. She was only seventeen when her father sacrificed her for the sake of having his gambling debts paid by Fittleworth's papa. You possibly know the story better than I. You are a contemporary of Fred's. Come to think on it, were not the two of you involved in an incident in your twenties, that had the militia pounding on the door of a well-known courtesan for disturbing the peace, and the two of you escaping out an attic window and across the rooftops? The more I ponder that, the more I am convinced it was you and Fred on that rooftop.

Regardless of Fred's lax moral code (and I am the last to point the finger, am I not?), he expected fidelity from his wife, and never got it. Were you one of her lovers? Oh, don't answer that! I don't care. What I do care about is the here and now, and Fanny mistaking Christopher for my lover. Was that a chuckle I heard all the way from Constantinople?!

That is not the worst of it. Fred thought so too. The plot thickens, because they both know Christopher as Cristoforo, having met him in Lucca when they were guests of Count di Nobili. The very same who is the husband of Christopher's Italian countess Maddalena. And so the Fittleworths were fully appraised of Cristoforo's role, which is why they thought we were lovers. The only good is that they never suspected he was my son.

So here was I with the famous Cristoforo as my house guest. And Christopher, knowing the Fittleworths from Lucca, played his part so well (too well as it turned out) that he was indeed transformed into Cristoforo, and I hardly knew him. I certainly did not recognize my son. The English, even the Fittleworths who have lived abroad for many years and consider themselves cultivated and knowledgeable about foreigners, have no understanding of the social position of a cicisbeo and thus they dared to view him through their English eyes as a male prostitute engaged by women of a certain age and social standing. Do you see where this is leading?

So to the incident.

I have put aside my quill to drink a dish of coffee because now, as I come to write out the incident in question it has made me reflect upon my past behavior, and the behavior of my circle, in particular your cousin Augusta. Forgive me for bringing up the past but I remember you telling me that in your youth Augusta preyed (I use the word deliberately) on you, and tried to seduce you, and this when you were a boy of fifteen or sixteen, and she almost thirty. Well, Christopher may be a man of thirty, with many years' experience of women, but the particulars are not far removed from what happened to you. So if the following narrative brings back painful memories, I ask your forgiveness. And if it makes you laugh heartily at the antics of this married couple, then laugh away. I do hope it is the latter.

So, what happened is this.

I was woken in the middle of the night by Fran, who in turn had been woken by my majordomo Carlo. And he in turn was woken by the noise coming from Christopher's bedchamber, of a woman and man in heated argument. At first we all thought it was Christopher, why wouldn't we? But then as we huddled in the passageway listening, it became apparent there was a third voice, much calmer than the other two, and that this was the voice of reason, and it belonged to Christopher.

Calling it a heated argument is putting it mildly. It was, in truth, a screaming match. She screaming at him and he growling back at her, all sorts of recriminations past, present, and future. Thank God my servants know little English, and even fewer foul words in our language. Though I was surprised that Fran, who I am very sure has never seen a man naked, least of all let one touch her virginal thighs, knew exactly what was being implied. So when the woman screamed that he was the "piss-proud owner of a lobcock so underwhelming she needed her spectacles to find it", my Fran turned white and her knees gave way. Carlo caught her before she fell to the floor (he did not manage to catch her a second time, and I will allow you to guess when that happened).

As you can imagine, I could have listened to this exchange all night for it was vastly entertaining. But then something awakened my mother hen instincts when I remembered this melodramatic squabble was taking place in my son's bedchamber. And you will be proud of me, because I then barged into his room without a second thought, and full of moral outrage, determined to rescue Christopher by ending the argument and sending the couple scurrying back to their own beds. Carlo, Sylvia, Fran, and the house porter followed close at my back. But I was only a few steps across the threshold when I came to an abrupt halt, which sent those behind me scrambling to a stop themselves and crashing into each other to avoid crashing into me. At the time, I had no idea, and I am very sure to an observer it would have been highly amusing indeed.

But the sight that presented itself in that room was enough for me to forget all other considerations.

Illuminated in the candlelight was Christopher in all his glory, sitting on the edge of his mattress, naked but for a handful of sheet strategically pressed between his thighs, and standing either side of him, Fanny and Fred Fittleworth, he in his nightgown and nightcap, and she half dressed, with her chemise falling off one shoulder. They were hurling accusations and insults at each other across my son's bare head.

To say I was in shock is an understatement. But it was when Christopher lifted his chin and his gaze locked on mine that I knew none of this drama was of his making. And when he gave an embarrassed half smile and rolled his eyes to the ceiling, it was not as Cristoforo, but as my son. That was all it took for my feet to become unstuck and I bustled forward, determined to end this high drama. But before I could utter a syllable to make my presence known, Fanny tugged the sheet out of Christopher's hand and began to climb up onto the bed, demanding her husband leave the room, that he no longer had her permission to be a spectator to her lovemaking with Cristoforo.

I heard a thud behind me. Later I learned it was Fran, who at the sight of Christopher standing in all his glory before he quickly cupped himself from view, fainted and fell, and Carlo failed to catch her. In my rage, I was oblivious to what was happening behind me. All I cared about was extracting Christopher from the Fittleworth fiasco, and so I went straight up to Fanny, and this will make you chuckle, I grabbed her by the hair and pulled her off the bed, she yelping and in no position to do anything but as she was told or be in more pain.

In an about-face, Fred came to his wife's defense and demanded I unhand her, which I did, but not until they were both well away from my son, who as soon as he was free of the couple scrambled to wrap the sheet about his body from chest to thighs.

I was in such a rage I could not recall precisely what I said to them. Christopher later told me. I reprimanded them for their disgraceful behavior and threatened to have them both thrown in the canal, and their belongings along with them, if they dared to trespass into my son's room again. Indeed, I said <u>my son</u> without a second thought as to whether Christopher would want me to publicly own to the connection. Though the dear boy did assure me that under the circumstances, he was very pleased I did. Is it not amazing, Roxton, how we as parents are quick to jump to our child's defense, no matter their age. It must be an instinctive response. I also told the Fittleworths that my son (there I go again!) was deserving of their respect, and they would treat him as a gentleman, which he was, and that was how he was always treated by members of the Tuscan aristocracy. And that if Fred wished to remain as consul and to have good relations with his Italian counterparts, he and Fanny had best forget this night ever happened, would not mention it to a living soul, and that if I heard one whisper about it, I would personally write to the Count di Nobili, who would see their disrespect and gossip as a personal affront to him and his wife, who had accorded Christopher the greatest respect while he lived as a member of their household. I then sent them off to bed with the directive that in the morning they would have the pleasure of meeting my son Christopher.

They slunk off, but not before both muttered apologies to Christopher and to me. I then shooed everyone else from the room, and when Christopher and I were alone, all the pent-up anger and outrage got the better of me and I burst into tears. For which he said he did not blame me, he felt like crying himself, which instantly made me feel better.

The next morning at breakfast, Christopher volunteered his side of the night's events. He had been sound asleep when something, he was not sure what, woke him, and when he sat bolt upright in bed, it was to find the Fittleworths standing side by side and peering down at him in the candlelight. Half asleep, he wondered if he were having a nightmare. That they were smiling at him only strengthened this belief. Then Fanny got into bed beside him without invitation to do so, saying she wished to avail herself of his services, and that she was sure he wouldn't mind if her husband remained to be a spectator. Christopher was about to disappoint them both, when apparently Fanny got the shock of her life when Fred said he had not come to watch at all, and fully intended to be a participant. To which Fanny was appalled, and the argument escalated from there.

I don't need to tell you that, had this not involved Christopher, I would have found it very amusing indeed to think Fanny was shocked by Fred's behavior and that he was shocked by hers. And when Christopher, who was now wide awake, and trying to be an intermediary for both husband and wife, was emphatic that he was not a body for hire in any capacity, neither of them believed him and this was the only fact upon which the couple agreed. And as they continued to argue, Christopher gave up any hope of a reconciliation and was hopeful their rage would soon burn itself out, when into his room I burst, along with my contingent of servant witnesses to the spectacle.

Should it surprise you to know that the Fittleworths cut their stay short by a week, and only remained a day and a night before they were off back to Florence? As they were both contrite and nothing else was said about that evening, we parted on civil terms, and Fanny took me aside and apologized for their behavior, adding that I was an exceedingly lucky woman to have such a handsome and caring son. I would have believed her sincere, except she winked and smiled at me in a way that now I am convinced that what she truly believes is that Christopher is indeed my lover and that I called him my son as a ruse to get them away from him! And do you know, Roxton, I simply do not care any more. I am reconciled with my son, and this incident if it has done anything, it has brought us closer together. I am off back to England as soon as Christopher sends word for me to follow him, and the Fannies and the Freds are unimportant to my future, and to Christopher's.

Give my love to Antonia, and if you do see Fred when next in Florence, I beg your discretion, though you have my permission to niggle him in that way you have that will see him squirm, but not know exactly why for.

All my love,
Kate

THE [FIFTH] DUKE OF ROXTON TO KATE, LADY PAGET

His Grace the Most Noble [5th] Duke of Roxton, Treat via Alston, Hampshire, to Kate, Lady Paget, Brycecomb Hall via Stroud, Cotswolds, Gloucestershire.

Treat
February, 1772

Kate, dear friend, are you sitting up in bed, or on your chaise longue? Whatever you are doing, wherever you are reading this, please do sit, for I have news to impart that will shock you. I do not want you taking a fall, or collapsing and hurting yourself.

Do you know what I have discovered? I am not infallible! You laugh heartily, but it is true that I am shocked by this. Indeed, I am not so lamebrained as to suppose that I ever truly was, but I did try to convince myself, if only so I could extend my earthly existence to remain here with Antonia, and with my boys, for as long as was physically possible.

Kate, I am dying. I have cancer. I do not know how much time is left to me. My physicians can only make guesses and predictions. Some are more morose than others. Some try to offer hope, when there is none. All look at me with concern for their own fine necks.

I kept it from Antonia for as long as I was able. But she knew. She said nothing and carried on, and still does, as if I will live into my nineties and beyond! It is not that she does not believe it is the truth, she just won't accept that I will die. You see—and I know you will snort with incredulous amusement at this—she does think me infallible. She always has. I intend to forever remain so, for as long as it is humanly possibly for me to maintain my dignity, all for her.

For how many years have we known one another? Thirty? Forty? For a handful of those years we were lovers, and I shall always cherish that time we spent together, just as I cherish our friendship. Antonia has always known—I keep no secrets from her— ironic for one of my disposition, who is secretive, close, and rarely demonstrative in public, to be unable to keep a single thought from her, nor do I want to. She sits curled in her favorite chair as I write this at my desk in the library, knowing I am writing to you, that I am slowly dying, and yet she never lets on to me or the family that she is crumbling inside to think she will not grow old with me; that I will leave her well before either of us is ready to be parted from the other.

As for you, my dear friend, my mind is easy, and I can leave you knowing you are being well cared for by your son. It pleases me beyond words that you and he are reconciled, and that he sent for you to live with him. I know how immeasurable was your loss when he was torn, literally, from your breast, as a suckling infant, and you were forced to return to society and leave him with your sister to raise.

And I ask your forgiveness for not having a full measure of your grief and loss at the time. Though I tried to be a good listener, to give you comfort and some diversion as your lover, and to offer you hope for the future (did I not foretell that one day you would be reunited with your son, and that he would know that you are in truth his mother?). Until I became a father myself, and held that most precious new life in my hands, a life Antonia and I created together, I had no true idea of what it would be like to have that all taken away from me. My heart ached, and I felt a stab of acute pain as I watched my infant son taking nourishment from his mother, to think you had to give up your infant at three months of age. Kate, please, forgive me my lack of understanding for your loss. If I could bow before you and kiss your feet, I would do so.

I won't write more here, but leave news and gossip for another more cheerful letter. And, Kate, let us not mention this cancer again. Let us carry on as we have always done, corresponding, exchanging gossip, and chuckling at the stupidity of others, while maintaining the façade that we will both be doing just this in ten, twenty, nay, thirty years hence. Believe me, that will make me feel a hundred times better than any words of comfort you could provide.

Write and tell me about your boy, and life in the Cotswolds, and how your sight is holding up. I shall begin a new sheet and a new letter, and write as a doting father and grandfather.

Until then.

As always, your beloved friend,
Roxton

CHARLOTTE, COUNTESS OF STRATHSAY, TO THE LADY MARY CAVENDISH

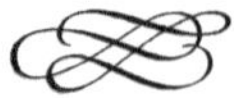

Charlotte, the Right Honorable Countess of Strathsay, Dower House, Fitzstuart Hall, via Denham, Buckinghamshire, to the Lady Mary Cavendish, Abbeywood via Bisley, Gloucestershire.

Dower House, Fitzstuart Hall, via Denham, Buckinghamshire
September, 1777

Dear Mary,

I have not heard from you in over a fortnight. I had your letter informing me of your return from Treat to Abbeywood, and that my granddaughter was again in her customary good health. I still do not understand how you could remain with Antonia while your daughter was under the care of that man whom Sir Gerald made her guardian. It is a disgrace he does not allow your child to visit with her relatives. Never mind she was unable to attend her uncle's wedding because of a head cold. She could have been brought along after the fact, not whisked away again by him to the back of beyond.

No doubt Antonia gave you her shocking news. I hope you were able to temper your incredulity and show the proper level of decorum and did not, as I am afraid you probably did, gush about her condition. We are all happy for her, naturally. But I cannot agree with any of it. It is beyond my comprehension why a woman almost fifty would want to engage in carnal relations, least of all with a lusty man ten years her junior, who would expect to exercise his rights in the marital bed, if not nightly, then often enough that it makes my stomach churn with revulsion. Being with child at her age is not only preposterous, it is embarrassing in the extreme, as well as dangerous. She should never have permitted herself to fall pregnant. It was beyond scandalous when she, as a young girl, married a man old enough to be her father, and now to turn around and marry a man ten years her junior, is just asking for trouble. I have always maintained, and I do not doubt it is unspoken amongst our relatives, that the reason her second son suffers from the falling sickness is because his father was an old man when he was conceived, and thus his seed was too old to give Antonia a healthy child.

So you can see why I am concerned lest Antonia now be too old to give her younger husband the heir he requires. There is the worry childbirth will not be easy for her, but of greater concern is that there are children born to older mothers who are not quite right in the head. Better it be stillborn than be born at all with such an impediment. Of course if that is the case, it won't be able to inherit, and that will be the end of the Kinross dukedom. More fool His Grace for marrying an older woman, when he should have looked to marry one ten years his junior if he wished with any confidence to supply the dukedom with an heir. But that man is not in the common way, either, is he?

Did it give you pause to feel resentful that your cousin at almost fifty is with child, when you, a woman twenty years her junior— indeed you were in your twenties for most of your marriage—was only able to produce one child in ten years, and that a female. With the birth of this child, Antonia will have supplied two dukedoms with heirs, no small feat, and only one such as she, who is blessed in everything she does, can carry off. Thank God the Roxton dukedom has a dependable and stable nobleman in the sixth duke. How a libidinous rake and an accommodating nymph produced such a son, who has a high moral code and a stolid disposition, is beyond my powers to figure. But they did, and well done them.

I am almost reconciled to your brother's bride. The new Lady Fitzstuart has her faults, and I am not referring to her being a cripple. I am still at a loss and wonder why such a vigorous healthy handsome man as Alisdair, who could have married any woman he fancied, set his sights on a girl with a clubfoot. His bride is far too frail and fragile, and I wonder if such a waif is capable of becoming pregnant, least of all bearing healthy children. And she must, because the Strathsay earldom's heir needs a legitimate heir. And if she can't produce one, the fault won't lie with your brother, will it, as he has produced a son already. And though I hate to admit it, and never would to him or to others, seeing the boy at the wedding I was reminded of Alisdair at the same age. He does have a great look of his father, so that no one could deny his paternity, though I dearly would love to do so, for propriety demands he not be acknowledged by good society. So why Roxton allowed him and his common grandparents at the ceremony still baffles me. In my opinion, the boy and his grandparents should not have been permitted into the church, but kept waiting outside with the servants where they belong, and which would have been perfectly acceptable to everyone. And did you see at the wedding breakfast how the boy brazenly came up to your brother's bride as if they were known to one another? She was most polite and handled the situation well, which showed her good breeding, and the boy's lack of it. I dare say I will be more reconciled to my new daughter-in-law once she is breeding and gives your brother a legitimate heir. And I do not doubt that she, as Shrewsbury's granddaughter, will surprise us all yet and may already be with child. And I must admit looks can be deceiving, for I would have thought someone with your robust health and child-bearing hips would have birthed five children in ten years, not just the one.

Let me turn to more pleasant subjects than your disappointing barren state and continued widowhood, which is a constant worry for your mother. Did you manage to speak to Antonia or Roxton about suitable suitors? It is high time you seriously made the effort to find yourself a husband. You cannot remain at Abbeywood forever. It does not belong to you, and never did. You have few prospects as it is, and your looks, such as they are, will fade with every passing year. You cannot be selfish and wish this state of affairs to continue, if only to ensure your daughter has a future, even if you do not. More I will not say on the matter.

This letter will reach you as I am making preparations for my yearly sojourn to Cheltenham for my health. You did not enquire in your previous letter about my health, which I must presume was an oversight on your part, and undutiful. For I always enquire after you and Theodora, and so it is only right and proper you do the same, particularly as you know I am never well at this time of year, what with the change in seasons. My rheumatism is worse, and made worse by the move to the Dower House. It is most callous of your brother to have tossed me out of my own home so soon. So I shall stay a little longer in Cheltenham to be out of the way of the repairs and work being done to the Dower House to make it as comfortable as possible. Your brother's bride did offer for me to remain at the Hall, but I declined. It is, after all, her home now, and I have no claim to it or anything in it. I have also declined anything of value, though she graciously said I could take whatever I felt would make the Dower House more livable. But no. None of it belongs to me, and so I shall relinquish it all

And before I forget, I do not need you to come to Cheltenham this year. Lady Fitzstuart's brother and sister-in-law, Lord and Lady Grasby, are in Cheltenham for her health. She too is pregnant, so at least Shrewsbury can look forward to his heir having an heir to follow him. And as Lady Fitzstuart is to visit Lady Grasby with her grandfather, they have graciously offered to go out of their way to Abbeywood, though why they would want to visit that part of the world, I know not, and they will bring Theodora to me at Cheltenham. So you see, there is no need, and I am very sure, no room in their carriage, for you to come along. I have no need of you, and Theodora at age ten is old enough not to need you either.

I expect a reply to this letter at your earliest convenience. And as you have very little to occupy your time, then I expect a reply very soon, and with the news that Theodora is eager to visit with her grandmother, and that you have made it perfectly plain to her that she is coming alone, and that her new aunt will be bringing her to me, not you.

Let me know in your letter how Theodora is progressing with her deportment and dancing lessons.

With a mother's love,
Charlotte Strathsay

*His Grace the Most Noble [6th] Duke of Roxton, Treat via Alston,
Hampshire, to Mr. Martin Ellicott, Esq., Moran House, the Bath
Road, Avon.*

Treat
Dec. 23, 1777

Dear Martin,

I trust you have your portmanteaux packed and are merely
awaiting my carriage to collect you, for after reading this short
missive, you are to be brought here post haste to share in our most
wonderful news and celebration.

Maman was brought to childbed earlier than expected—and on
winter's solstice night, of all nights!—and was safely delivered of a
daughter. I have a sister! Mother and babe are very well indeed,
and as you can imagine, the great weight of worry I have been
carrying throughout her pregnancy has lifted. Why I never feel this
way with Deb, except with the onset of her labor pains, I must put
down to my wife's bountiful good health and uneventful pregnancies. For which I thank God, for it seems we are destined to have a
large family, and that suits us very well indeed.

But you know, do you not, mon parrain, more than anyone else alive, that Maman's pregnancies have been anything but uneventful.

As expected, Kinross is beside himself with happiness and relief to have his duchess out of danger, and to again be a father. And as both parents were desirous of a daughter, their greatest wish has been granted. It has worked out rather well that Kinross is a duke in the Scottish peerage, for my baby sister will one day inherit the title and be a duchess in her own right, for according to Scot's law it is not the eldest son but the 'heirs of my body', thus any child, and not whether the child is male or female, which determines who is a Scottish nobleman's heir. I know you will be as happy as we are with this most satisfactory and fitting outcome for Maman's daughter.

Thus my baby sister begins life with the grand title of Marchioness of Leven, heir to the Duchy of Kinross, beloved by her ducal parents, sister to an English duke, and also to the son of a duke. Her life is blessed from the start. She is of robust health, cries lustily, and has a head of dark hair that reminds me of Frederick at birth.

While her nephews and nieces have yet to make her acquaintance, I know they will be just as besotted as her parents and her brothers.

Little Lady Leven is yet to receive her Christian names, as Maman and Kinross are still negotiating those between them, but I am hopeful that by the time you arrive and I am assured before the christening takes place, she will have a string of pretty names to call her own.

I shall leave this here, for I cannot wait for you to join us and meet the newest member of our family.

Love,
Julian
R xo

EVELYN GAIUS FFOLKES, EARL OF STREATHAM ELY, TO THE LADY MARY CAVENDISH

Evelyn Gaius Ffolkes, the Right Honorable Earl of Streatham Ely, to the Lady Mary Fitzstuart Cavendish.

[Not dated but believed to have been written some time before December 1777. A handwritten note attached to the folded parchment states: Given in person by Her Grace the Duchess of Kinross to her cousin the Lady Mary Cavendish.]

My dear sweet Mary,

You will always be my first love, and the love of my life. You do know that don't you? I have had many lovers. I even thought myself in love and tried to elope with Deb, and this before I had any knowledge she was already married to Julian, and I do love her, too. And I was married for a time to a harmless pretty creature who deserved better and who died trying to give me a child. And yet, my heart, this blackened emotionally shriveled organ, if still beats at all it beats for you and always will.

Nothing has changed since we were fourteen and we shared our first and only kiss. I wish I could have saved you from a loveless marriage to that pig swill Gerald. Aside from not marrying you, my greatest regret in life where you are concerned is not having the bravery to put you out of your misery by taking Gerald's life. So many times did I rehearse how I would kill him, and yet, I did nothing. By the time I could, I was a prisoner in a faraway land, unable to offer you anything but prayers. That Gerald shot and killed himself is a fitting end for such a pig of a man, and as far as I was concerned, could have happened sooner. Perhaps, had he still been living when I was finally at my liberty, I would have found a way to end his miserable existence to free you.

My thoughts shock you, but they do not surprise you, do they? You have always known and forgiven me my selfishness, my self-absorbed passionate nature, and my immorality. I know I am the most selfish and immoral person I have ever encountered. In short I am not a nice person. I am hateful at times. I have no conscience and my morals are questionable. No wonder Shrewsbury recruited me! For I am an excellent spy, am I not? I have done things, horrible things, all under the blanket of doing them for King and Country. Such things would make you cry and despair of me. But I had no conscience about doing them, and would do them all again, if asked to do so. It is as well then that I have no wife or children to weep in despair at my depravity. In truth Dominique's death in childbed was a blessing for her and our child.

My only saving grace is my music. To think I can compose music so sublime it stirs the senses leaves me in awe. That I can no longer play what I compose on the pianoforte or my viola with my usual brilliance after having lost partial digits through my nefarious activities is fitting punishment is it not?

But I lie. I have another saving grace. Surrendering you to a better man.

I could make you a countess, give you whatever your heart desires, and you and I could flit about society in our silks and perfume, everyone in awe of us, and we would be happy, for a time. But you deserve more than what I can provide. You deserve a man worthy of you. And so you will marry your handsome squire and be blissfully happy, my dearest Mary.

Christopher Bryce is everything I am not. The only thing we share in common is that we love you body and soul. He is honest, moral, brave, truthful, honorable, and I see that he loves you with all his heart. I would not let you marry a lesser man. He will make you an excellent husband, and be an exemplary father to your daughter Theodora, and to the children you will give him. And you will bear his children, of that I am convinced. You both deserve one another, and I wish you every happiness.

Please, dearest Mary, do not cry for me, worry for me, or think of me at all. Live your life with your squire. Light a candle on my birthday if you so wish, but that is all you are to do. I shall live my life as best I can, and in the selfish way I have done for so many years now that it is the only way I know how to live, or want to live. There was a moment of madness when I thought I might be able to settle, to live as you do, as my peers do. But that is not to be. Do not think I will ever forget you, or my family ties. But I shall continue my interest from afar. Will we see each other again? Of course, my darling. But I cannot say when, or under what circumstances. I hope it is before I am old and stooped and of no use to anyone.

Do give my regards to Silvanus (your squire will know what I mean, and I do mean it with affection).

I kiss your fingertips and what love I have to give is yours, always.

Eve

MR. CHRISTOPHER BRYCE TO THE
[SIXTH] DUKE OF ROXTON

Mr. Christopher Bryce, Brycecomb Hall via Stroud, Gloucestershire, to His Grace the Most Noble [6th] Duke of Roxton, Treat via Alston, Hampshire.

Brycecomb Hall via Stroud, Gloucestershire
July 8, 1778

My dear Duke—Roxton,

The Lady Mary has delivered me a son and heir. A rather curt announcement that in no way expresses how I am feeling at this moment, and no doubt will continue to feel for the foreseeable future. I never expected, though I had always hoped, to become a father, just as I never expected but dreamed of one day marrying your cousin. That both have now come to pass has me as dazed as the day you shook my hand and welcomed me into the family, and acknowledged me as kin to your dearest wife. That seems a lifetime ago but less than twelve months has passed. And if I may be so bold as to add that since that first visit to Treat, I have come to know you better (indeed I did not really know you at all before then, did I?), so that it seems, to me at least, we have been friends all our lives. I hope that you feel as I do.

Forgive me. I have had little sleep over the past three days since my son made his entrance into the world, so that I do not doubt I am wasting ink in writing down the ramblings that are swirling about in my head. I know my news is not news to you at all, for I sent a short missive to Her Grace your mother announcing our new arrival just hours after his birth. Yet I wanted to write to you privately, under separate cover, to share my thoughts, as a new father, with one who so generously shared his wisdom with me on becoming a father, and most importantly, on how I was to conduct myself during my wife's labor, should she wish me to be with her at such a time.

She did indeed want me with her, which filled me with a mixture of relief and terror. But I am proud to report I remained beside my dearest Mary throughout the entire ordeal, following your advice to the letter. And thanks to your sage counsel, I managed to keep my tongue between my lips until asked to speak, accepted in silence the verbal abuse my dearest wife threw at me when she was in the most pain, and offered encouragement when it was safe to do so.

I do not mind telling you, and perhaps this attitude will change over time, but I do not think I could go through such a traumatic episode again with the same stoicism. I am a coward when it comes to seeing my dearest heart in such distress. Yet what mighty creatures females are to be able to endure the pain and torment of childbirth to deliver us new precious life. Did I shed a tear? Most definitely. And I tell only you because you were generous in confiding in me that you have done so at the births of all your children.

Thank you for sharing your wisdom and for giving me your confidence. And may I be the first to congratulate you on your suspicion (which I am sure is now confirmed) that you are to be a father for the sixth time in the new year. I will await your dear wife's letter to Mary before I am suitably surprised to learn the news.

To tell you a little about our infant, he has inherited his mother's glorious coloring. It is a family trait, is it not, with your son Lord Augustus having a head of red curls, and Mary said her grandmother (who is your dear mother's grandmother, also) was famous for her red hair. And though there was no portrait of the Countess of Strathsay at Treat for her to show me, there is one hanging at Fitzstuart Hall which I will be sure to seek out when we visit.

All being well with Mary and the babe, we mean to travel into Buckinghamshire at the end of summer to spend a month at Fitzstuart Hall as guests of Lord and Lady Fitzstuart, so that our families can become better acquainted, and we will meet for the first time their infant twins. I mention them here because Her Ladyship wrote to Mary that while her son has a head of black hair just like his father, their daughter has fair hair that may indeed be a shade of red. Such news was music to Teddy's ears and she is determined to start her own club amongst her relatives with price of admittance being, you guessed it, the possession of a head of red hair, or a shade of that color. I believe two of your progeny will have instant admittance.

You can imagine then Teddy's response when she learnt that her baby brother has a shock of red hair. She was more excited about this fact than she was having a brother, which is what she most wished for because she will be able to teach him to climb trees and to ride a pony, so, as she put it "David and I can go a roamin' at our leisure"! Did that make you chuckle as much as it did me, Your Grace?

I shall leave you shaking your head at your niece's exuberant pronouncements to return to my wife's side, where I hope to hold my infant son and stare at him in contented stupefaction, as all new fathers must, at the miracle of life.

Yours & Sincerely,
Christopher

C. Bryce

PS. You enquired about the wool yield of a Cotswold Lion, as well as the possibility of breeding the lion with perhaps a Leicester ram in the hopes of improving carcass quality. I shall mull the latter over and write to you about this and the other matters you raised under separate cover. As for the former, a ewe can produce an annual fleece of about twelve pounds of white wool. As you see, fatherhood has not turned my brain completely to mush... yet!

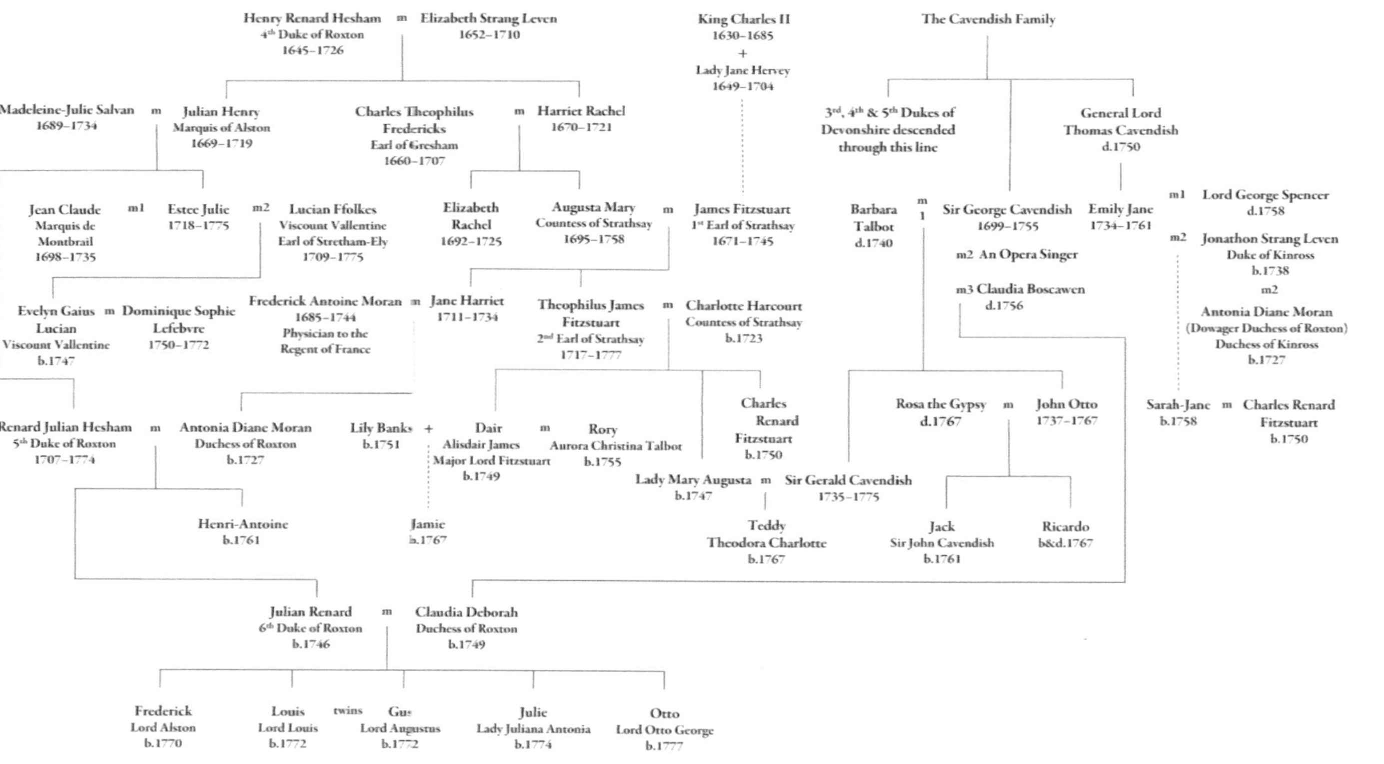

Henry Renard Hesham m Elizabeth Strang Leven
4th Duke of Roxton
1645–1726
1652–1710

King Charles II
1630–1685
+
Lady Jane Hervey
1649–1704

The Cavendish Family

Madeleine-Julie Salvan m Julian Henry
1689–1734
Marquis of Alston
1669–1719

Charles Theophilus m Harriet Rachel
Fredericks
Earl of Gresham
1660–1707
1670–1721

3rd, 4th & 5th Dukes of
Devonshire descended
through this line

General Lord
Thomas Cavendish
d.1750

Jean Claude m1 Estee Julie m2 Lucian Ffolkes
Marquis de
Montbrail
1698–1735
1718–1775
Viscount Vallentine
Earl of Stretham-Ely
1709–1775

Elizabeth
Rachel
1692–1725

Augusta Mary m James Fitzstuart
Countess of Strathsay
1695–1758
1st Earl of Strathsay
1671–1745

Barbara
Talbot
d.1740
m 1 Sir George Cavendish
1699–1755

m2 An Opera Singer

m3 Claudia Boscawen
d.1756

Emily Jane
1734–1761

m1 Lord George Spencer
d.1758

m2 Jonathon Strang Leven
Duke of Kinross
b.1738

m2

Antonia Diane Moran
(Dowager Duchess of Roxton)
Duchess of Kinross
b.1727

Evelyn Gaius m Dominique Sophie
Lucian
Viscount Vallentine
b.1747
Lefebvre
1750–1772

Frederick Antoine Moran m Jane Harriet
1685–1744
Physician to the
Regent of France
1711–1734

Theophilus James m Charlotte Harcourt
Fitzstuart
2nd Earl of Strathsay
1717–1777
Countess of Strathsay
b.1723

Charles
Renard
Fitzstuart
b.1750

Rosa the Gypsy m John Otto
d.1767
1737–1767

Sarah-Jane m Charles Renard
b.1758
Fitzstuart
b.1750

Renard Julian Hesham m Antonia Diane Moran
5th Duke of Roxton
1707–1774
Duchess of Roxton
b.1727

Lily Banks + Dair m Rory
b.1751
Alisdair James
Major Lord Fitzstuart
b.1749
Aurora Christina Talbot
b.1755

Lady Mary Augusta m Sir Gerald Cavendish
b.1747
1735–1775

Henri-Antoine
b.1761

Jamie
b.1767

Teddy
Theodora Charlotte
b.1767

Jack
Sir John Cavendish
b.1761

Ricardo
b&d.1767

Julian Renard m Claudia Deborah
6th Duke of Roxton
b.1746
Duchess of Roxton
b.1749

Frederick
Lord Alston
b.1770

Louis
Lord Louis
b.1772

twins

Gus
Lord Augustus
b.1772

Julie
Lady Juliana Antonia
b.1774

Otto
Lord Otto George
b.1777

SATYR'S SON LETTERS

THE [FIFTH] DUKE OF ROXTON TO LORD HENRI-ANTOINE HESHAM

His Grace the Most Noble [5th] Duke of Roxton to Lord Henri-Antoine Hesham.

[Believed to have been written in December 1772, and given to His Grace's twelve-year-old son upon the Duke's death in early 1774.]

My dearest boy—my son,

To my great sadness, I will not live to watch you grow into the fine young gentleman I already know you are. I never wanted to leave you. I never wanted to spend a day away from you. And I never regretted a single moment with you, watching over you, and being by your side whenever you needed me to be there.

Maman and I waited many years for your arrival, and when you finally came we were happy beyond words. You have given us such joy. You are so wanted and loved. Please never forget that.

I wish I could have held on to life for that little bit longer, to look after you, to protect and watch over you, and to help you better understand that there comes a time in everyone's life, from the crossing sweep to His Majesty, when we must pass from this earthly existence into the next, to be welcomed into the kingdom of heaven. But to do so means leaving our loved ones—leaving you—behind to live without us.

Please excuse your papa for one moment while he wears his ducal coronet from beyond the grave, to advise you, his son, of his four maxims: Strive to control your emotions when in the public gaze. Love and laughter are to be reserved for the privileged few. Arrogance is a nobleman's prerogative, but a true gentleman chooses to be humble when the circumstance calls for it. Never forget you are my son; others won't.

I am chuckling as I write this, for I am certain you are rolling your eyes and sighing and wish to complain to your dear papa that you know these maxims well enough, and that you have not forgotten them, and are not likely to ever forget them because I have told you them often enough, particularly before our visits to Versailles. And yes, you have always done Maman and me very proud. So! Enough of papa's lecturing.

Though I do have one last favor to ask of you, and that is for you to keep this thought with you at this time: None of what is happening around you—my passing, Maman's grief, Julian's sadness—is your fault.

Did I not tell you many times that my illness had nothing to do with you? And this you must believe because it is the truth. What is also true is that your life, the life you knew when your papa was well, will never be the same again. For the longest time you will be sad. That is only natural. And for the longest time, Maman and Julian they will not be themselves. It is perfectly acceptable for you to shed tears and to wonder if the world has gone a little mad.

But I promise you that as the years go by, and you grow taller and stronger, life will return to some semblance of normality, and you and Jack (who is the best friend you could possibly have) will be carefree again and live life to the full.

That is what you must do, for me, for Maman, for Julian, for Jack, and most importantly, for yourself—live, and enjoy your life. I know that you will never forget me, that I will not be far from your thoughts, and that there will be times, quiet moments, and moments of stillness, when you will feel an oppressive weight upon your chest of unbearable sadness. You will sob until it hurts to breathe, and you will wonder why life could be so cruel as to take your dearest papa away from you too early.

And how could your papa possibly know what it is like to feel abandoned and lonely, as if cut adrift and floating directionless on rough seas, and everything around you is a vast dark ocean, and all because your papa is not there by your side to steer you to a safe harbor?

I know this because when I was your age I lost my own dear papa, and in the most tragic of circumstances. I became adrift in this vast dark ocean. And while the circumstances of his passing are different, the experience was no less harrowing, and in some respects—and this you may not wish to believe because how could your grief be surpassed?—it was far worse, because of what happened after he died.

So I wish to share this experience with you by telling you a final story. How could your papa leave you without one last tale to tell? You were a most excellent listener and audience to your dear papa's fantastical tales of his misspent youth, whether told to you in the English or French tongues. Those hours you lay on the couch recuperating afforded me the leisure and the opportunity to recall my many adventures, and to reflect on my life, and I thank you for that opportunity.

So indulge your dear papa while he tells you about himself when he was twelve years old.

For this story I will call myself Renard, which is the name my parents gave me, and the name Maman calls me when we are private. This will make it easier for me to relate such traumatic events, for while your brother and Martin know of this episode, I have only shared my inner most thoughts and the details with your Maman. Now I wish to confide them in you. I hope too that when you are older, perhaps many years into the future, when you come across this letter, you will read this story again and you will have an even greater understanding, and thus appreciation, of why I confided it in you.

The story begins over half a century ago, in Paris, at our hotel on the Rue St. Honore. Here Renard lived as a boy with his parents and baby sister. In other respects it was like our family too. Parents who loved one another with a son who was an only child for many years before another sibling arrived to surprise everyone. And with the arrival of the baby, many visitors came to the house bearing gifts and to coo over the infant. There were parties and fetes at home, and day trips into the countryside to take the infant to meet aging relatives.

Renard loved his baby sister, but he was sullen that she should receive so much of his parents' time and the attention of these important relatives. His papa saw this, and wished to make amends. So one day, when his baby sister was about nine months old, his papa offered for Renard to accompany him on the week-long hunt in the forests of St. Germain. But Renard's mama would not hear of it, saying the hunt was too hazardous and no place for a boy. Was Renard's papa out of his mind? He had only one son and heir. It was enough that she had the worry of her husband risking his neck, without her son risking his as well.

No matter how loud and long Renard pleaded to be allowed to accompany his papa, his mama would not change her mind. Renard said that if his papa truly loved him he would take him along, regardless of his mama's objections. But his papa would not yield, and told Renard that remaining with his mama and baby sister was for the best; was he not the man of the house when his papa was away from home? He must take care of his family until his papa's return.

Renard was not to be appeased and he spat out that his papa did not love him at all. For good measure he declared that he hated both his parents equally. Renard was to regret those words for the rest of his life.

From a window high up in the hotel, Renard watched the activity in the stables courtyard as his papa and his men readied themselves. Stable hands prepared the horses, and a carriage was loaded up with servants and supplies to accompany their master on the week-long adventure. He saw his mama come out to farewell his papa, and his papa give her and his baby sister a kiss of farewell. His papa then looked up to the window with a smile, and waved. But Renard was so embarrassed to think his papa knew he was there all along that he scrambled away without waving back. And when he rushed back to the window, regretting his petulance, his papa with his men were off under the archway and out of sight.

It was the last time Renard saw his father alive.

Renard's papa died on the hunt, taking a fall from his horse and breaking his neck. It was a swift, painless death, and he was gone, just like that, within a blink of an eye, leaving behind an inconsolable young wife, a twelve-year-old son, and an infant daughter. And now Renard, at twelve, was head of his family, and his mama and baby sister were his responsibility. But he was not given much of an opportunity to exercise this new-found maturity, for just three months after his father's death, while the family were still in deep mourning, strangers arrived at the hotel in the dead of night, to take Renard away to live with his grandfather in far-off England.

Renard's mama, her French family, and their lawyers were powerless to stop this. With his papa's death, Renard was now heir to his English grandfather's dukedom. And because he was heir to this dukedom, his grandfather had rights over him. Renard had never met this old man, he knew very little of the English tongue, and he had never visited the country of his father's birth. But most importantly of all, he had never been away from his mother.

This meant nothing to the strangers who had come from England to collect him. Renard was taken forcibly from his home, from his mother's arms, in fact. The servants fell about in fits of despair and his mama howled like a wounded animal as her son was dragged away and bundled into a carriage. Renard kicked and screamed and tried everything in his power to be free of his jailers, but to no avail. He thrashed about in the carriage, determined to escape, and when they could not stop his hysteria and calm him with words, these men fell upon him, he a thin slip of a boy, and beat him until he was still. He was then tied up so he could not move at all, and a cloth pushed between his teeth and bound about his head so he could no longer make a sound. Terrified, Renard wet himself, and he was so ashamed to have lost control of his dignity that he fainted. When he woke, he found he had no tears left to shed and fell into a stupor from which he never fully recovered.

With his father dead, and separated from his mother and baby sister, Renard was no longer surrounded by love and cocooned in a warm happy place. He was forced to live with his ancient grandfather, the fourth duke of Roxton, who was a cold, bitter old man unused to the company of children. This old man was a stranger, and Renard hated him. But he was smart enough to realise that he need only bide his time, for it could not be many years before his grandfather died, and then he would be duke, and no one would be able to tell him what to do. And when he became duke he would return to France, to his family, and he would never leave them again.

Renard bottled away his grief, but in so doing he bottled away his heart, and any love that he had to give. But as there was no one to receive his love, or to give him love, it was an easy adjustment to make. He mentally put his heart in a jar, and locked it away in a cupboard deep inside himself.

The old duke lived for another seven long years, and in those years Renard was forbidden to speak or write in French, and to have any contact with his mother. The old duke wanted his grandson to be an Englishman, to forget his father and his French maman, and to forget the life had lived in Paris. Renard was sent to Eton and to Oxford, and when he inherited the dukedom just after his nine-teenth birthday, he was in every respect an English duke, of which his old grandfather could be proud.

You must wonder how Renard could possibly forget his French heritage, his mother who loved him, and the life he had in Paris with his parents. But you see, my dearest boy, without love, without the warmth of his parents, and with the loss of his dear papa, something of Renard—your papa—died inside him. And when I became duke at such a young age, I decided that I had no need of the heart I had stored away in a jar in a cupboard deep inside me, for having a heart had only ever caused me great sadness.

I lived in this way, without love, and without a heart, for almost two decades. It was Maman who found that cupboard and unlocked it, and it was she who found the jar with my heart in it, and she set it free. It was her love and her belief in me that made my heart beat with love again. And since that day, I have wondered how I lived so much of my life without it.

Your dear papa tells you this tale, my darling boy, not so you will be sad for him, but because he knows that to live without love is not to live at all. It was wrong to keep my heart in a jar. It was wrong to lose all hope and to despair. It is better to have loved and to feel loss, than not to have loved at all. You must grieve, and you must feel the loss of me so that one day in the future, when you find the love of your life, you can love and know great happiness and accept the love of another freely. This, too, you must do, for your maman, who loves you so very much, and who, after a time of mourning, will be there for you, always.

I promise you that one day, not today, or even tomorrow, but one day, when you are a young man, all this will come to pass. You will have to trust your dear papa about this.

I also told you this story about the young Renard so that I may apologize to you, for leaving you, just as my papa left me. Though my papa did not have the luxury of saying his farewells. I trust that when the day came that I finally had to leave you, you were far better prepared than I ever was. And no one will ever tear you away from your mother, your brother, and your family. You will always have them. You will always have a home here at Treat. And you will always be surrounded by people who love and care for you. Of that I give you my word and solemn promise.

You are not to worry if you shed tears over this letter, or even if you are so angry at me for leaving you that you scrunch these pages into a ball and toss them on the fire. If it will make you feel better, do so. This is a copy of the original I have left with your brother, for safekeeping. He is charged with giving you the originals of all my letters upon your twenty-first birthday.

Your papa needs to rest now. And I have written enough in this letter that I hope it gives you some comfort, and for you to know that you have not heard the last of your dearest papa! He will have more to say in his next epistle. Until then, he remains—he forever remains—your dearest loving papa.

R

THE [FIFTH] DUKE OF ROXTON TO
LORD HENRI-ANTOINE HESHAM

His Grace the Most Noble [5th] Duke of Roxton, to Lord Henri-Antoine Hesham, on attaining his majority.

[Believed to have been written in December 1772, before His Grace's death in early 1774, and held in trust by his successor and His Lordship's brother, then given to His Lordship on his 21st birthday; seal broken 1782.]

My dearest boy,

Congratulations on reaching your majority.

I remember your birth as if it were yesterday, when I held you in my arms that first time, your maman and I so overjoyed and overwhelmed to welcome another son into our lives. And so I am exceedingly happy to be sharing this most special of anniversaries with you via this letter.

Your dearest papa told you many years ago that you had not heard the last from him, and so here I am to be with you for this short interval. I may not be able to kiss and hug you, but know that I am most definitely with you.

But I do not write from beyond the grave to unsettle you, or to stir up painful memories of my passing, but in the hopes that in the intervening years since your dearest papa had to most reluctantly leave you, you have lived your life well, and been happy. I do not doubt you have grown into a fine young gentleman of which I can be very proud.

I trust that you and Jack spent a few years at Oxford and that now you are planning, or perhaps you have already set off on your tour of the Continent. You will have the most marvelous adventures, and bring home many memories, and hopefully a collection of art and curios worthy of gracing the walls and cabinets of your rooms.

I discussed your twenty-first birthday with your brother, and it was agreed that on this day Julian would present you with the keys to your own apartment at Treat. It was something we both wanted to do for you, and it has been in the planning since I first became ill; an architect engaged to refurbish part of the east wing to allow you to have your very own apartment. I trust you are pleased with the result. It was our wish you have autonomous living quarters, much in the French manner, so that you may come and go as you please, and live as you please under your own roof. And while I always wanted you to have a home at Treat, I must tell you that the decision ultimately rested with your brother, as sixth duke, to allow you this grace and favor residence within his home, and the home of his children. I could not have hoped for you to have a more loving and caring brother. Knowing these plans were well underway by the time of my final illness, and that you would always have a place to call your own within your childhood home, did much to ease my worry about your future.

It is your future that I most wish to talk to you about in this letter. And you will forgive your papa for mentioning it, but mention it I must, because your affliction will always be so much a part of you. I know that even to this day it governs much of your day-to-day choices, and as much as you or I or your maman or your brother wish it were otherwise, it is so and cannot be ignored. And thus we must deal with it as best we can. I am confident you are doing just that, and with exemplary fortitude and forbearance.

Since you were very small, your maman and I were aware that you were special, and would never be like other boys. The falling sickness precludes you pursuing the normal opportunities open to the sons who will not inherit their father's title. Not for you a career in the army or navy, most definitely not the clergy, and the law or politics would not suit either, not because I do not believe you clever, for I do, but for the simple reason that such professions require you to be in the public gaze. I would not wish that on any man who possessed a shy nature, least of all one debilitated with the falling sickness.

And I trust that over the years you have ordered your life in a way that suits you, treating your affliction as a trifling inconvenience requiring adjustment, rather than living a life as its slave. For while it will always be with you, you cannot allow it to consume you. It should always be a puzzle worth solving, rather than a burden you must shoulder.

And because you are special and cannot follow the usual vocations open to second sons, you are in the enviable position of not following in any footsteps, or fulfilling any expectations. But I also realize that this leaves you adrift. Your papa is going to bring you into a safe harbor, but in doing so he will complicate your life by informing you that now, on this your twenty-first birthday, you have come into a vast inheritance.

I had hoped to be here for this day, which I began planning for just after your fourth birthday, when it became apparent you would never live a life free of seizures. Each year since that day I have set aside a portion of my yearly income earmarked for your inheritance. This was then invested in the funds, and I continued making these yearly deposits until your brother inherited the title. I did my sums, and with eight years of accumulated wealth, and invested until you turned one-and-twenty, I should think that on this, the day of your twenty-first birthday, your inheritance is a little over one hundred thousand pounds. £100,000. I have inked it in numerals as well, in case you thought your dearest papa must have been in his dotage and added that hundred in there by accident.

Congratulations. You are now an exceedingly wealthy young gentleman. There are no strings or stipulations, or overseers, for this wealth. It is all yours from this day to do with as you see fit. Yes, you may gamble it away, spend it away, use it on all manner of trinkets and vice, women included, and there is not a thing anyone, including your brother, can do about it. You could also hoard it and be miserly with it, or perhaps you feel guilty having such wealth and wonder if you should not press it all on your brother, who I am confident now has a large family, all of whom he will need to provide for in some form or other from his wealth and estates.

Let me assure you that your brother inherited vastly more than any man, even with a large family, estates to run, and hundreds of retainers to care for, would ever need in five lifetimes. He is wealthy beyond measure, as was I for most of my life. My grandfather, the fourth duke, was a miser. If he spent a penny, it was on accumulating more pennies. The only thing in his life on which he lavished his attention and wealth was Treat, in building works, the house and grounds. He did this to fashion it into a monument to himself and his name. He employed a slew of architects and landscape gardeners, surveyors, skilled artisans, and hundreds of workers, but labor, as you know, is cheap and so cost him very little. Materials also were as nothing, when the stone came from his own quarries, and the natural resources from lands in his possession. So when my grandfather died, he left behind no one who mourned his passing, only a half-finished palatial carbuncle on the landscape called Treat. I saw fit to complete it and I hope I was able to turn it into a home for your maman, and your brother, and you.

While your brother may lift his eyebrows in surprise at the amount of your inheritance, he would never begrudge you any of it. And if he has any concerns, it will be with the fact that I have not placed any restrictions on your access to it; your brother cannot withhold it from you, nor is he able to portion it out to you, which I am certain he wishes he could do in your best interests. I do not doubt that you thank your dearest papa for this, but perhaps you will not thank me when I tell you that with great wealth comes great responsibility. Your one hundred thousand pounds is now upon your shoulders, and while I do not want to weigh you down, it is there, and now it is for you to think long and hard about what you wish to do with it, and your life. For the worth of a great inheritance is measured not by how it is kept, but in how it is spent.

I have given you a unique opportunity to make something of your life, something that goes beyond the bricks and mortar of a great palace or securing the future of an illustrious title. That is your brother's burden to bear. As my eldest son he was denied any other way of life. On you, on the other hand, I have placed an altogether different type of burden, and this is one of choice.

Your dearest papa has great confidence that you will, as always, conduct yourself and your life in a manner that will make him proud, and I have always thought that you will surprise me, and go beyond the expectations of others. You are, after all, my son.

With this letter is a small box, and in that box is a gold ring, set with a carnelian stone carved with the family coat of arms. It was my father's ring. He wore it every day of his life, and I remember this ring as being part of him. I did not wear it myself, having inherited the Roxton ducal emerald ring that was my grandfather's, and which all dukes of Roxton by tradition wear upon coming into the title. I do not doubt that your brother now wears that ring with pride. However, this ring, the one I leave to you, has great sentimental value for me, and so I wish you to have it, to remember me by, and as a symbol of a love between a father and his son. I loved my father very much, indeed I adored him, and I know that you in turn loved me just as fiercely.

I think your dearest papa has given you enough to think about for one letter. As I write this, I know you will visit me at my tomb and show me the ring and how well it fits your finger, and I cannot wait to see you there.

Oh, and if you think this is the last you will hear from your papa in ink, it is not. But that other letter which I left behind we shall leave for another day. Which day? I cannot predict, but I do so hope that day does arrive, and in the not too distant future, and that you will indeed feel the need to open it and read what your papa has to say upon that occasion.

I love you with all my heart.
Your loving dearest papa,
R

MARTIN ELLICOTT, ESQ., TO LORD HENRI-ANTOINE HESHAM

[*This correspondence included with gracious permission of Their Graces due to its significance in shedding light on the establishment of the esteemed Fournier Foundation. Names and passages supressed in the usual manner at their insistence.*]

Martin Ellicott Esq., Moran House, the Bath Road, Bath, Avon, to Lord Henri-Antoine Hesham, Treat via Alston, Hampshire.

Moran House, the Bath Road, Bath, Avon
May 12, 1784

My Lord,

Dear boy, I received your letter by this morning's post and it cheered me immensely. I have no real reason to complain, what with the spring weather being superb. My breathing is better today than it was last evening, and a long letter from Her Grace your mother yesterday always has the power to cheer me, and more often than not, I am laughing out loud before the end of the first paragraph.

My health is as precarious as the changing weather so I will come straight to the point lest I have a coughing fit or it rains, or both.

You know His Grace your brother wishes for me to spend what is left of my life at Treat with the family, and I am greatly flattered by his offer. But between us I cannot leave [*suppressed*] here, not after twenty years' [*suppressed*] [*suppressed*], and [*suppressed*] will not come to Treat. This despite His Grace extending his invitation [*suppressed*]. We would not be comfortable with such an arrangement, despite Their Graces (and when I say that, I do mean not only my godson and his wife, but include your dearest mother and Kinross) assurances that we are equally welcome. When I die, and I say when, not if, because it cannot be far off, then it will be here, with [*suppressed*] by my side. [*suppressed*] is aware, however, and is reconciled to the fact that once I leave this emaciated carcass behind, I leave [*suppressed*] too, because I mean to return to your father and the home that was mine almost from birth. To be interred in the Roxton mausoleum is an honor I value beyond price. Your family is my family and has been since my parents were in the service of your great-grandfather, the fourth duke. To know I will forever be near your father and, in time, your mother, is a great comfort to me, and it seems it is so with your brother, with you, and with Her Grace your mother. [*suppressed*] understands this and respects my wishes.

The honor your family does me cannot be adequately put into words, and if I tried to do so I know the writing of this letter would take twice as long, if it would be finished at all. I am so overcome with emotion it is crippling.

I must thank you for your kind offer to allow [*suppressed*] to remain here in this house that has been our home for the past sixteen years. But we have jointly decided to accept His Grace's equally kind offer to [*suppressed*] of a townhouse in the center of town, within a stone's throw and a sedan ride from the King's bath. That [*suppressed*] will have a place to call home and an income for life has set my mind at rest. I have written to His Grace under separate cover of our wishes in this regard, and to thank him from the bottom of our hearts. And of course, I cannot thank you enough for allowing us to remain here after you inherited the estate from your esteemed parent. I trust one day, when you eventually marry, that you and your bride will fill this house with as many happy memories as we have.

You may find this morbid, but it is necessary to impart. While I have bequeathed my savings and worldly goods to [*suppressed*], I am leaving my art collection and my library to you. I know you will appreciate these the most. And you at least will not take offence that amongst my collection accumulated over decades, from my time with your father and later during my Continental travels with your brother, there are volumes, paintings, and cartoons considered by those who cannot appreciate art for art's sake, or are too prudish in nature to even contemplate such artworks or even open such books, as beyond what is decent. For instance there is a complete set of miniatures by Boucher, and another by Fragonard of [*suppressed*] and [*suppressed*]. I also have in my collection a rare statue of the nymph and satyr enjoying [*suppressed*]. Amongst the folios is a set of the works of the Comte de [*suppressed*], and another by Mme (or so she calls herself) [*suppressed*] which I know you will enjoy more for the wit in the prose than any salaciousness contained within the pages. I also have left you what I believe is one of only two copies of [*suppressed*]. Your father presented this to me upon my retirement, and of course he had the other copy. There is also [*rest of the paragraph suppressed*].

Enclosed herein is a detailed listing for your perusal, so that when you come here, or you send your representative, after we are gone, you will find everything as we left it, with the paintings still upon the walls, the statues in my closet, and the collection of cartoons in marked folios along with the books in the library.

[*List available but not included in this work.*]

Let me turn to more cheerful and far more important matters.

I am honored you seek my advice on your venture to establish a medical foundation to aid physicians with their research endeavors, and for the advancement of medical science. I approve the name Fournier Foundation. Such a name suitably distances you, the son of a duke and brother of one, from the, dare I say, murkier aspects of the medical profession. You and your family's name must remain above reproach, given there are those amongst our medical pioneers who are conscienceless when it comes to the procurement of specimens for dissection and investigation, resorting to the use of the still-warm bodies of those wretched persons who have forfeited their lives on the gallows. And, I can scarcely believe it possible, that these physicians accept the cadavers from freshly-dug graves, the bodies stripped of their clothes and presented naked to the anatomy schools, where they are subjected to all sorts of bestial treatments in the name of science. Stealing clothing and possessions from the dead is an offence, but not, it seems, the naked dead bodies of these poor souls. I understand our medical men need to be able to poke and prod at the human body to be able to learn the secrets of its internal workings so as to help the living, but surely there are better, more respectful ways of going about such explorations?

Never mind my objections and pontifications. You must do what you see as fit and proper and worth the investment to aid in the advancement of scientific knowledge. But I do caution you to keep yourself at arm's length from the day-to-day particulars of such a venture. Nor am I completely at ease at the prospect of you visiting places rampant with the miasma of disease, particularly given the delicate balance of your constitution. Please take heed and always think of your health first and foremost. Your mother could not bear the loss of you; it would cleave her heart, and not even the love of Kinross could bring her back from the brink of such despair.

Allow Dr. Bailey and the other trustees to step in and make such visits on your behalf, I beg and counsel you. Bailey as your choice as the foundation's figurehead is a most excellent one, for I always found him to be of a curious mind and compassionate disposition. And dare I suggest you bestowed the title of Director upon him most generously because of your intimate association with him when he was your personal physician when you were a boy. I think mayhap you wish to make amends for your highhanded treatment of him, and his good-natured acceptance of your youthful arrogant nobility. I mention this with the deepest respect.

Your desire to remain the anonymous benefactor is a most circumspect decision. If it were publically known you had loosened your purse strings on this venture, all manner of trencherflies and patronage seeking ponies would be beating at your door, with any number of ludicrous schemes and pleas, that I do not doubt you could employ a full-time secretary just to deal with such petitions alone. Remaining in the shadows will allow you greater freedom to distribute your largesse where you see fit. Having a board of trustees to assist you is a necessity, but do not allow them to govern you. Though now that I have penned that in ink, I am smiling, because I can think of no one other than you, with the exception of your esteemed parent, who was less likely to be governable or persuadable by others once his own mind was fixed on a decision.

Your dearest father would be immensely proud of you, and how even at your young age, you have taken the wise and most generous path to use your inheritance to make a difference in the world. And I do not doubt you will, and for not just the few but for the many, indeed perhaps thousands upon thousands of our nation's most vulnerable souls most in need of medical care and attention, and the myriad of hopeful possibilities the advancement of the science brings with it.

You have inherited your mother's sharp intellect and thirst for knowledge, but also her compassion for her fellow creature, for why else have you chosen to do all you can to improve the human condition by establishing a medical foundation to help the poorest of poor wretches, if not because, like your dearest mother, you possess great empathy? And while you have a great look of M'sieur le Duc, your temperaments are also closely aligned, and I am not referring to your father's great arrogance or natural aloofness with those outside his immediate family circle. I knew your father well, and he could not hide from me that he was a man of deep feeling.

This was most evident with your mother, for no greater love have I seen than that betwixt your parents. And the love he bore you and your brother was beyond measure. And as one who has known you from the cradle, it is my belief that you are a perfect balance of both your parents, even more so than your dear brother. Not that I would confess that to him, and this will remain between the two of us.

If you will indulge an old man to offer you some advice. While I know you do all in your power and what your wealth can provide to cloak your affliction from society, and I heartily agree with your judgment in this, for it is nobody's business but your own, when you find a mate, when you fall in love, surrender yourself to her completely, as your father did with your mother. He never hid his true self from her, nor should you hide your affliction from your chosen bride. It is part of who you are and will always be thus. And if she loves you, as she must, completely, as your mother loves your father, then you will have a long and happy marriage, and that is what I most wish for you, love and happiness, and to be loved is nothing less than you deserve.

You are the kindest, most generous, and feeling man I have had the privilege to watch grow into a fine gentleman. Please do not weep for me, for I am done with this old, tired, worn-out body and, to be truthful, and I keep this from [*suppressed*], I am counting the days when I can leave this mortal prison of wasting flesh and am free to be reunited with your father, and be by his side once again, and forever.

With love,
Martin

Miss Theodora Cavendish, Brycecomb Hall via Stroud, Gloucester-shire, to Miss Lisa Crisp, c/o M'sieur de Crespigny of Fournier Street, Spitalfields, London.

Brycecomb Hall via Stroud, Gloucestershire
July 8, 1784

Dearest, <u>dearest</u> Lisa,

This is my second letter sent to your Fournier Street address, and I promise you it won't be my last because I am determined, yes <u>determined</u>, to find you, my Blacklands sister.

I cannot believe I have left horrid Blacklands behind forever, and returned home to the blissful Cotswolds. I have never been happier to be home with my family, to watch my darling baby brothers grow into boys, and to be able to hug Mama whenever I wish it, and to go out riding about my beautiful, beautiful countryside with my dear papa. All is again right in my world, and I never want to leave here ever again. But I cannot be completely happy until I know you are safe and well, and you send me a reply to one of my letters. I am finding this silence between us unbearable and if I were not with my family and in my beloved Cotswolds, and, as I told you in my previous letter, betrothed to my Jack and making plans to wed him, I think I would take to my bed and never leave it until you came to free me from my melancholy.

At the very least, here at home I am able to write freely and as often as I like, and both my parents understand that I must write to you, and why it is so very necessary that I find you. For I cannot, I will not, marry my Jack without you at my side.

I cannot remember if I told you before this letter, but I was forbidden to write to you from school. That isn't strictly true. I wrote you many letters, it's just they were never sent because it was thought in my best interests that all ties between us be severed. But I will never ever ever give up on you my dearest, dearest friend in the entire wide world.

My heart is breaking, Lisa. I still do not understand why you left me without a word of your departure, with no farewell between us. Was our parting all too much for you to bear that you thought it best to up and leave without saying your goodbyes? How could you be so cruel? I do not want to believe you would be cruel to any living thing, and most definitely not to me, whatever others might try to persuade me otherwise. I won't believe them! Ever. I know they are only trying to be helpful in telling me to forget you, but tell me how that is helpful? We were as close as two sisters who loved each other could be, sharing each day, and our secrets, well, my secrets because you do not have any and are too good to have any, and then one day you were gone, just like that, as if you had never been there at all.

I thought you had died. No one would tell me. No one would mention you. I was ordered not to ask about you because I was upsetting the other girls with my continual questions. But what about my feelings and how upset I was when you vanished? Did no one think I would be? I am still upset, and no matter how many years go past, I will never stop wondering and worrying and wanting my Lisa returned to me. Others at the school were also upset, so it was not only me you upset by leaving without a word. George, the carpenter's son, and his father, too. Signore Baldi, and little Daisy, Mrs. Frank's daughter from the sewing room. But none of them could tell me what had happened to you, and all assured me you were most definitely not dead because no one had been carried out in a casket, and no one had mentioned a death.

They, I mean Mlle Bromley, Mlle Martin, and the grand dame of our esteemed Blacklands, Mme Girouard, or as I always called her when we were private, and which made you giggle, Maîtresse Grandes Bajoues. They all assured me you were not dead, but said it was for the best that I think of you as dead, because it was not as if we would ever see each other again. And when I contradicted them and said I had every intention of seeing you again once I left Blacklands, and that I would never ever forget you, Mme Girouard sat me down and told me with a perfectly grave face that I was very special, but that you were not. She said, and you must pardon the insult because it is what she said, not what I believe at all, that you were so far beneath me in social consequence that I might as well be living in the clouds, and you in a ditch, for that was how far apart we were and would forever remain. And because of this great gap that would never be closed between us, we were destined to tread very different life paths and lead very different lives. She is an utter trencherfly, all because Uncle Roxton is a duke and mama is the daughter of an earl, and she would have loved to have said as much, but because she was always lecturing us at morning assembly about loving thy neighbour and treating everyone as we found them and showing Christian charity to all, she could not, could she, because she wasn't being charitable at all. Quite the opposite. She's such a hypocrite.

I pretended not to understand her at all and pulled that face I used on Mlle Martin when she would ask me if I knew what had happened to the extra slices of cake, and I would shake my head and ask her whatever did she mean? When all the time the cake was in my pocket. And who could blame me for taking what was rightfully ours anyway? She certainly did not need anymore of our cake. Poor Lisa, you found stolen cake hard to swallow did you not? But we still ate every crumb because they never did give us enough to eat at supper!

I had some satisfaction in watching Mme Girouard tie herself in knots as she tried to explain the differences in our social consequence as the natural order of things, and God's will, until I had had enough of her squirming and her Janus-faced explanations and just burst into tears to get her to stop. Though, my darling Lisa, the tears were very real, as was my frustration, because I miss you so very very VERY much that my heart hurts.

Dearest Lisa, I mean to persist in writing to you until there is no ink left in the whole wide world and you write to me and tell me you are well and safe and that you miss me too.

For now I shall close this letter by kissing the page, and telling you that I have not forsaken you! Papa is traveling into Stroud for a meeting of clothiers or some such, and I want him to carry this with him and send it from there with the coach.

Love you to bits, my darling dearest Lisa. I remain your best friend in the whole wide world and your Blacklands sister forever,

Teddy

[Translated from the French.]

November 6, 1784

Dearest Papa, I lost another part of me today. We received news (which surprised no one because we have been waiting for it any day now) that Martin passed away peacefully in his sleep two days ago. He was not in bed but outside on the terrace in his favorite chair, tucked up snugly and enjoying a *café au lait*. Jeremy thought he was dozing, he looked so peaceful. I am glad he went this way, and pray he is already with you, and you have embraced your confidant and friend and welcomed him into Heaven to be at your side. I cannot see for my tears and I fear I will splash my words, but I do not care. I am bereft. It is as if you have died all over again and I must again endure the pain and heartache of that loss. I know I shall feel this way until he is brought here to be interred. That at least will bring me some consolation, having him near, with you, and with us.

I go up to London at the end of the month, after Martin's interment, to meet with the medical men Bailey recommends I appoint to the board. I think you will be pleased with his choice for our foundation, which goes on apace with many more applications for funding than we can possibly satisfy. Such is the sorry state of the medical care in this country.

Today I accompanied Julian over to Alston, and Freddy came with us. We showed our faces at The Swan. The locals do like to see their duke and his heir out and about. You would be proud of your grandson, who is turning out to be a fine young man aware of what lies ahead of him. He is almost as serious as his father, though no one could be as serious as that, could they?! But I predict Freddy will follow in his father's footsteps and be an exemplary duke, which will please you. I, on the other hand, spend my time when I am upright and capable of it, in frivolity, so I, too, am doing my bit to keep your legacy alive! Ha! Was that a raise of your eyebrow in displeasure? Surely not! I kiss you and leave you, my health no better or worse than it was yesterday. xo

Miss Theodora Cavendish, Brycecomb Hall via Stroud, Gloucester-shire, to Miss Lisa Crisp, c/o M'sieur de Crespigny, Fournier Street, Spitalfields, London.

October 28, 1785

Dearest Lisa,

Yesterday the most marvelous idea sprang from my head! I am exceedingly excited and think myself very clever to have had such a thought. I confided in Mama and she thinks my idea might just work! She has encouraged me to write to see if it could be done. I hugged her so tightly both of us almost lost breath. I am happy to have a plan, but I am also happy for another reason, and must tell you our family's news before I continue on to tell you of this plan of mine.

Last evening at dinner, Mama and Papa made the most marvelous announcement imaginable. We are to welcome an addition to the family in the new year! Not a person, silly. A baby. A baby brother or, if I could keep my fingers crossed for the entire time to ensure the outcome I would, though Mama suggested I pray for the outcome too, and that's to have a baby sister join our family. Indeed! Mama is enceinte and is due in the new year. It was a surprise to her and Papa as much as it was to Granny Kate and me. My brothers are excited, of course, but have no notion that the baby will not be here until February, which for them might as well be a hundred years from now. I predict that every day they come down to breakfast, they will ask if the baby has arrived. And when my baby sister does finally make her entrance into the world, her crying and fussing will have them running out of doors as fast as they can manage it.

But just because we are to have another baby in the family, and, if wishes can come true a girl, does not mean I will ever forget my Blacklands sister. Which is why I have come up with the most marvelous plan to have you found.

Do you remember me telling you at school that I have powerful relatives who love me? I am sure you must. It is these powerful relatives I will enlist to find you, for what is the good of powerful relatives if they cannot help me? And Mama assures me they will help, and not deny me my wish.

If there is one person in this world who can grant wishes, it is my Mama's cousin, Mme la Duchesse d'Kinross whom I like to think of as my fairy godmother. It is her eldest son who is the Duke of Roxton, and it is his wife, the Duchess, who is my aunt. Mme la Duchesse d'Kinross will find you. I know it. She would do anything to aid in my happiness, and she will apply to her son, my Uncle Roxton, to employ what methods they have between them to discover your whereabouts.

How difficult can it be when I have your last known address? Mama believes, like me, that the Duchess will do everything in her power to assist in finding you, particularly as I have told her I want you, and <u>only you</u>, to be my bridal attendant. How can I marry Jack without having you there by my side?

So confident am I that the Duchess will find you, that I am less melancholic and much more hopeful. Mama says it has brought out my smile. For although the thought of having a baby sister did make me feel so much the better, I won't feel myself until we two are reunited.

I leave off writing now, my darling dearest friend, because I must turn my concentration to writing to Mme la Duchesse d'Kinross. Unlike my letters to you, which I can keep private, I will have Mama read my letter to Her Grace, because I want it to be perfect, and I want her help.

I mean to also give Mme la Duchesse your invitation to my wedding, which can be delivered along with this letter when she finds you, and she <u>will</u> find you!

Your dearest most special and everlasting friend and Blacklands sister,

Teddy

DEBORAH, DUCHESS OF ROXTON, TO SIR JOHN CAVENDISH

[Undated but delivered the night before Her Grace's nephew's wedding to Miss Theodora Cavendish, July 1786.]

Dear Jack,

I wanted to write you this letter about my thoughts on this the eve of your marriage so that you may keep it always. Know that, even as you embark on this the next chapter in your life as a married man, with all the responsibilities and joys that entails, and in the not too distant future, adding to that of being a father to your own family, you never lose the love and worry of your mother. For that is what I have essentially been to you since your own dear parents were taken from you at such a young age.

I have always strived to do my best for you and to show you the love and protection of a mother, even when still in my teens I had no real idea of what it was to be one. But, do you know, giving birth to my first son, and with every subsequent birth, I am still learning what it is to be a parent. I have always thought of you as mine own and included you in that number.

For you are, in many ways, my first-born, even if I did not give birth to you. I have loved you, protected you, given you shelter and guidance, and worried over you, and you have never disappointed me, or any member of our family. I am so proud of you, of the boy you were, and of the man you have become.

You have a great capacity for compassion and for love. And as a fellow musician, I can hear those feelings conveyed in your compositions. It is not surprising that your pieces often move your audience to tears. Those feelings are not only revealed in your music, but in how you treat others.

You are the greatest friend Harry could ever wish for, and you are as close as brothers could ever be. I know his parents, and his brother, are so thankful that you came into Harry's life when you did, for I do not doubt they feared he would never make friends, such is his self-absorbed and melancholy disposition. But given his affliction, that is understandable, is it not? Still, you have been a most loyal friend and his champion, and I greatly admire you for it.

And as we are speaking of self-absorption, I must ask your forgiveness for my own distraction. I have the excuse of pregnancy and the birth of eight children in ten years, as well as the responsibilities that are attached to my position as wife and as duchess to your Uncle Roxton. But that does not make me any less aware that upon my marriage I let slip my mothering duties where you were concerned and allowed you to drift along in Harry's company, the two of you with intermittent supervision, particularly in the transition period between the death of M'sieur le Duc and when your Uncle Roxton became duke.

I hope you know that I was and I am here for you, always.

You have from time to time asked for my advice, and I hope I have always given you sound counsel. I hope too that you will continue to seek me out when you require the opinion of someone who is detached from your household but who will always provide you with honest opinions within a framework of love and guidance. You are your own man and I respect that. But even men are still worried about by their parents, particularly their mothers, who will always see them as their little boys. So do forgive me if upon occasion I wish to receive a hug and a kiss from my eldest boy. I do not think I will ever <u>not</u> want that, therefore you must show your dear Aunt Deb forbearance. I trust you will hug and kiss your children long into their adulthood, too.

I am so proud of you, Jack. And I say without reservation that your parents, particularly your father, who was the most wonderful brother a sister could have, loved you beyond words, as I do. I see a lot of your father in you, and I do not mean just his musical talent. He, too, had a great capacity for understanding and love. It has always been my great privilege to be able to watch over you, to love you, to see you become your own man, and a gentleman my dear brother Otto, your father, would have been so proud to call son.

I know you will make Teddy a wonderful husband, that you will be a loving father, and that you both will live a happy and fulfilling life. If I can offer you one piece of advice about marriage… At the end of the day, when candles are snuffed and you are alone together, it is as if only the two of you exist in the world, and that is as it should be. Be kind and loving with one another; nothing else truly matters.

All a mother's love,
Aunt Deb

THE [FIFTH] DUKE OF ROXTON TO LORD HENRI-ANTOINE HESHAM

His Grace the Most Noble [5th] Duke of Roxton's letter to Lord Henri-Antoine Hesham, on his decision to marry.

[Believed to have been written in December 1772, seal broken July 1786.]

My dearest son,

So you have found the love of your life and are to marry. Congratulations. I am exceedingly happy for you.

I do not doubt the girl who has captured your heart is someone special indeed. You would not settle for less, nor should you.

Shall I tell you about her? She is unique. Beautiful. Accomplished. Clever. These are words that come to mind when I think of her. She is your intellectual equal. She makes you smile for what you believe is for no reason at all. You laugh together. You feel slightly drunk in her presence, and more than a little bit in awe of her, of how you feel, of this new-found situation in which you find yourself, because for the longest time you just did not believe you would ever find someone like her. Above all else, you can be yourself with her, and there are few people in this world that we ever truly trust with our true selves. But you trust her, and thus are totally at your ease. There is no artifice, no pretense, no urge to impress or be impressed. The two of you could sit on a chaise longue all day and not say a word, and yet that is the point, is it not? Words are sometimes unnecessary to convey feelings. Just being with her, being in each other's company, is enough. You wonder if you will wake up and it will all have been a dream, this feeling, this girl, the future you desperately want to share with her and no other. But it is not a dream, my son, and you will spend the rest of your life living this dream—with her.

How do I know this? Because this is precisely how I feel about your maman, and have felt about her almost since the day we first met. I shall tell you about that day, but first your papa has some words of wisdom about marriage he wishes to share with you. And again it begins with your dearest maman.

You have a mother who is learned and loving, and for whom feelings are everything. Your parents were devoted to one another their entire married lives. And you have a brother who, in spite of his marriage being arranged, is very much in love with his wife, and she with him. I am confident these examples of wedded contentment have surely provided you with all the proof you need that it is possible to fall in love, remain in love, and live a loving and fulfilling life with the right partner by your side.

For that is what a marriage is, my dearest boy, a partnership of love and mutual respect, and it is a commitment for life. I dare to hope that it also extends beyond this mortal body of mine to an eternal life, so that I will once again be with your mother when her time comes, and she will be able to join me.

But a marriage is only successful if both parties are wholeheartedly invested in the union, emotionally and spiritually, and on equal terms. It will not work any other way. To live it half-heartedly would make life intolerable. You would become a burden on each other, and both feel caged. It would be something from which you wished to escape. And why would you not? And husbands can. I have seen this time and again with my fellows. The wife is forsaken, they take a mistress, sometimes they live with one, and do whatever is necessary to remain outside the cage of their marriage. I do not judge them. I cannot. For the longest time, before I met your maman, I was part of such a precarious and hollow existence, and thought little beyond it. But with great age and many years of reflection, I can assure you that as much as I enjoyed those years unfettered, nothing equals a life shared with your soul mate. Nothing matches the life your mother and I shared together, and the life we shared with you and your brother, as a family.

But your papa does not mean to lecture you on marriage or love, merely to offer you some personal reflection. You have made your decision, or you would not have opened this letter…

Or I dare to hope that is the case, and that you are not reading this as an afterthought, an afterword to your own life spent as a sad, cynical old rake who never found love, or more tragically, let the love of your life slip from your grasp because of your pride and vanity, or some such notion you allowed yourself to believe to excuse your regret. My hope is that you found the love of your life many years before I did, so that you will have so many more years together than I was able to share with your dearest maman.

Let me tell you a secret, that is in truth no secret at all. I was at the precipice of spending my life precisely as I have just described, as a sad, cynical old rake, when into my life stepped (or should that be twirled?) your maman. At the time I was not sad, and I did not think myself old. I was, however, most decidedly cynical. Nor did I have any desire to change the way I lived. I was a great libertine who had bedded every willing female who took my fancy; there was good reason I was given the moniker 'the noble satyr'. As you are now a man and not a boy, and quite possibly have had your fair share of bedroom escapades, I can confide that while I enjoyed these encounters—indeed some of my lovers have become my life-long friends—they provided me with physical gratification only.

Any emotional connection was fleeting, or not of a depth to alter my feelings. It was not until I met your maman that I realized that not one of my lovers had truly engaged my heart.

Do you remember me telling you in a previous letter the story about the cupboard where I stored my heart in a jar when I was a boy, and how your maman found this jar? Indulge me while I recall how your maman released my heart from its captivity, only to capture it for herself. There is a point to this, I assure you.

I will always remember the first time I saw your maman. It is as clear to me today as it was almost thirty years ago. I was with a group of friends strolling the gardens of the palace of Versailles. I remember who I was with, my mistress of the moment and our friends, and a number of French nobles, but I do not recall the topic of conversation. I do know that the day was overcast, and there was a hint of rain, so there was talk of returning indoors. And then, as if the clouds had parted and the sun had come out, there she was, your maman, walking straight towards me. I stopped. I stared. I forgot the sentence that was on the tip of my tongue. Time slowed. In my distraction, the heavens could have opened and rain poured down upon me for all I cared, or knew, of my surroundings. Your maman was the most beautiful creature I had ever set eyes on, and, believe me, that is no small boast for I was always surrounded by beautiful women. But with her, there was something, something I could not quite fathom at that moment, but it went beyond mere physical beauty. She was and still is the most beautiful woman I have ever had the pleasure to admire, but there was so much more to her beauty. You see, she also radiated sunshine, and all that was good with the world. In truth, she radiated love, and always has.

Of course, I was so befuddled I did not understand what was happening to me. And for the longest time I was disbelieving, that I, the noble satyr, had been struck down in my thirty-seventh year by Cupid's arrow. I refused to entertain the notion that I could possibly have fallen in love with a girl, for she was not much more than that. She was only twenty (though she fibbed about her age to me, for she was in truth barely eighteen), and I believed her too young for me. I resisted what my heart was telling me, and more importantly, what your maman knew to be self-evident. Our love was fated. We were meant to be together. That was all that mattered. The opinions of others were unimportant. Any and all objections were void, and this included my great reluctance because I considered myself too old to marry her.

I did my utmost to ignore my heart, using excuse after excuse as to why I should not follow my feelings, and marry your maman. Of course, in the end, she prevailed, and I thank God daily I succumbed!

The point is, my dearest son, no obstacle is insuperable, no excuse plausible, and you should never second-guess yourself when the heart is involved. Believe what that most determined organ is telling you. Rejoice in the feelings you are experiencing, and be confident that all that truly matters is that you are fallen in love, and that you marry the love of your life. It is meant to be.

I give you further proof of fate with the enclosed, a wedding band. It belonged to my mother, who married my father when she was sixteen and he twenty years her senior (the irony of history repeating itself cannot be lost on you either). They married against the wishes of her family, and his. She a Catholic, he a Protestant. And she married him at great personal cost, for her family disowned her, as did her church. And yet, despite this, they married and remained in love until the day he was cruelly taken from his family after a fall from his horse broke his neck. I told you about this also in an earlier letter, you may recall, so I will not say more on that painful subject. My mother never remarried, and remained faithful to my father's memory for the next fifteen years, until she was finally reunited with him after her own death from pneumonia.

So it gives me great joy to bequeath you the wedding band that once belonged to my mother, your grandmother, Madeleine-Julie Salvan Hesham, Marchioness of Alston. It is a symbol of my parents' love and commitment against all the odds. I now pass it to you to present to your bride as your symbol of love and commitment to her, and to one another. I know that she will wear it with pride, and hold it as dear to her heart as did my mother.

I will offer up one final secret, something of which you possibly are now aware, so that it is no secret at all, for surely with this letter, how could it be? Your maman has always known it, as does your brother, who is also a great believer, though he thinks he inherited it from Maman. I believe he received a dose from both of us. I am just as sentimental and as emotional, and as great a believer in fate, as is your dearest maman. I hope, no, I am certain, you are too.

Marry her, Henri-Antoine. With the love of your life by your side you can achieve anything you put your mind to. You will live an extraordinary life, one that is full of happiness and wonder, and contentment. But most importantly of all, it will be a life full of love.

Bring her to meet me. I cannot wait to be introduced.

I love you with all my heart, my dearest son, and wish you a life-time of joy.

Your most loving papa,
R

SIR JOHN CAVENDISH TO MISS THEODORA CAVENDISH

[*Written in a feminine hand on the obverse is the sentence: Delivered to me at the Gatehouse Lodge at first light the morning after the incident on the cricket field.*]

July 1786

Dearest Theodora,

I wish to apologize for my appalling behavior of yesterday. What must you think of your soon-to-be-husband to be getting himself into a brawl with his best friend, and in front of everyone. I know what Uncle Roxton and Aunt Deb think. A sad, sorry fellow who deserves to be pulled by the ear, sat in the corner, and given a good tongue-lashing. And that's exactly what happened. And I deserved every word of what Uncle Roxton threw at me, and while this left me miserable, which was as it should be, I had no defense against Aunt Deb's disappointment in me. She tried not to tear up, but she did and I saw it, and was made even more wretched.

Aunt Deb is as close to being my mother as it is possible to be. I don't remember my own mother at all, only Aunt Deb, who tucked me up in bed, read me stories, and soothed my fears that there were no monsters waiting to jump out of my clothes press as soon as the candle was snuffed. It was she who first encouraged my love of music and saw my potential, and was the first to show me how to hold my bow to the strings of my little violin. And do you know, Theodora, when I reflect upon it, I marvel at how she, at the tender age of just seventeen, took me under her wing and treated me as her own chick. I could have been shuffled off to other distant relatives, even sent away to boarding school, but no! She would have none of that and was determined that I should have a mother and a home. And then she married Uncle Roxton when I was nine, and I felt I had both a mother and a father for the first time in my life.

After you, Aunt Deb is the person I love most in this world, and I owe everything that I am to her. And while I spent most of my youth by Harry's side, it was to Aunt Deb I turned to if I was feeling ordinary, and wanted a motherly hug or some reassurance all was right with the world.

And how do I repay her mothering kindness, and Roxton's care and attention? By punching and knocking Harry to the ground and making myself a disgrace! That's how. I've never felt a greater fool, or a more ungrateful ass. I have disappointed her, Uncle Roxton, my family, you, my darling dear, and Harry. Lord save me! How has it come to this that I punched my best friend so hard it sent him into a seizure? Most of all, I loathe myself for acting in this manner before you, and almost on the eve of our wedding. And here was I thinking everything was coming along swimmingly.

Thinking about it as I sit here practically roped to Uncle Roxton's chair, at his desk, to write this handful of apology letters to everyone that matters, I made a startling discovery. Do you know, I think I have loved you since we first met when you were ten. Not in that way, silly. Not then. I first loved you as a cousin, and then as a friend. I remember thinking that you were the bravest girl, indeed the bravest *person*, I had ever met. Aside from Harry—who deals daily with his affliction, and that is brave in itself, isn't it?— you shimmying up trees and galloping all over the countryside, fearless and as one with nature and animal, flitting about with your sunny smile and love of life was beyond anything I had seen before in a girl. You took instantly to Nero, and he to you, and you couldn't stop giving him cuddles and praise, and that's how you took to me, too, and my viola playing! You never said an unkind word about my wish to compose music, you were always interested and listened to me drone on, and play on and on, as if I were the most accomplished person in the entire kingdom.

You were so different from other girls that I didn't even think of you as a girl to begin with. Don't laugh! You know very well what I mean! And for the longest time I thought of you as a friend, though I did wonder even then if we might suit and marry and end our days as a happy couple. And then you kissed me that day under the oak. That was a bit of a wake-up for a fellow like me, who had never kissed a girl, and yet you kissed me. The most awful thing was, it woke me up to the fact you were a girl all right! And then when you told me you were going to marry me, instead of laughing that off (as Harry did when I told him) I was secretly happy you thought as I did. From that day I could think of no one else with whom I would ever wish to spend the rest of my life.

You do know that I love you to the moon and back, Theodora, don't you? I love you. I love you. I love you. I LOVE YOU.

Had you not kissed me that day, I still think I would have woken up to you soon enough because you are the most beautiful, the most delightful, the most accomplished girl I will ever know, and I love you even more today than I did back then under the oak, and even more than when I asked you to marry me.

I know that our marriage is what everyone wants, and they tell us it is the perfect union of two branches of our family. Everyone approves of it, don't they? But even if they didn't approve, and even if we weren't cousins, I would still want to marry you, and only you.

And I'm not just saying this to get back in your good book after yesterday! So don't think it, Theodora. I'm telling you this from my heart. I had wanted to keep it for our first night together as husband and wife, but I'm telling you now, in ink, so when we do go up before the parson, you know I am doing so not to unite our families, but because you are the only girl for me, and with whom I want to have babies and spend the rest of my life.

I know I'm a distracted sort, head in the clouds and all that with my viola-playing and music-making and creating, but never forget that while that is a big part of my life, you and only you make my life worth something. I write my music for you. I will be a parliamentarian for you. I will be the best husband and the best father to our children, all because I love you. In truth I would do anything to make you happy.

Can you forgive me yesterday's aberrant behavior? I will not sleep tonight worrying that you think less of the man you love than you did yesterday. I will hate myself if you think me nothing but a brute and a brawler and a care-for-nobody.

I can't explain precisely what happened out there on the field, only that Harry said something ungentlemanly to your best friend and it made my blood boil over. Never mind he was angry, and he and Miss Crisp were having a heated argument, he should never have said what he said, and so I lashed out, wrongly, but I could not help myself. Again, I have no excuse, but it is done now, and all I can do is move forward and ask everyone's forgiveness.

I am bursting to marry you, my Theodora, so please, please, _please_ forgive your Sir John his stupidity, and say you will still love me as much as I love you, and that you will become my Lady Cavendish the day after tomorrow.

This letter is sealed with a kiss and a great heap of worries only you can smooth away.

Your ever loving,
Sir John

*[An extract, not the entire entry, for that day.
Translated from the French.]*

July 6, 1786

Renard, today Henri-Antoine became engaged to be married. Did you, like me, ever think this day would arrive? You would approve of his choice. Lisa is a darling girl and naturally she is very beautiful. She would have to be, would she not, to pique Henri-Antoine's interest. Ah! But to hold and keep it, and make him want only her, required that she be very special indeed. And she is. She is intelligent, unpretentious, honest, and forthright. Her French tongue it is very good. She reminds me of a swan, unconsciously gliding through life with an innate confidence and grace. She is also devoid of artifice. This and her modesty are the qualities that most impress Julian. Is that not to be expected? Deb is just like this, too. And for a nobleman in his position Henri-Antoine needs a wife who does not flatter him in the least. But best of all Lisa has an inner beauty, a beauty that shines out from within. That is a rare quality for a woman who is beautiful, yes? Something you always said of me. And like you, our son would not have fallen in love with her without it. She also has strength of character and purpose, is full of optimism, loving, and did I tell you she is oh so clever!? Yes, of course I did. You see how happy I am that I repeat myself!

Lisa's start in life was not so good, and as a poor orphan she has defied all the odds. I admire her for that alone. I tell you with confidence that she is truly worthy of her elevation to wife of the son of a duke, and not just any duke. She is worthy of being *your* daughter-in-law, and worthy of *our* son.

She loves Henri-Antoine unconditionally, and is his most fiercest champion and protector. Knowing he now has the perfect mate has enabled me to breathe so much easier. For that alone I will always love and cherish her. Naturally Henri-Antoine is besotted with her, which is as it should be, and in that too he is like you. I do not doubt that when they are alone together he truly is himself with her, in every sense... Even in those moments when he is gripped by his illness and has no control, he trusts her to be by his side, and you know he has not trusted anyone for such a very long time I despaired of him ever doing so. And now Lisa is in his life, and I am so very happy. Renard, they are truly perfect for each other, and so in love...

MISS LISA CRISP TO DR. AND MRS. ROBERT WARNER

Miss Lisa Crisp, c/o His Grace the Most Noble Duke of Roxton, Treat via Alston, Hampshire, to Dr. and Mrs. Robert Warner, 9 Gerrard Street, Soho, London.

[*This letter, along with other correspondence pertaining to the Fournier Foundation, was generously donated to the Roxton archive by Miss Wysteria Warner, youngest daughter of Dr. and Mrs. Robert Warner's only son, the distinguished surgeon and Fournier Foundation trustee, Dr. George de Crespigny Warner. Written in ink on the obverse is the sentence: Delivered by His Grace's personal courier, and a response sent by Dr. Warner within the hour.*]

c/o His Grace the Most Noble Duke of Roxton, Treat via Alston, Hampshire
July 1786

Dear Dr. Warner and Cousin Minette,

I write from Treat to let you know I will not be returning to Gerrard Street.

I know this will come as a great shock to you both. But I assure you nothing untoward has happened to me. In fact I have the most wonderful news to impart, and I hope you will be just as happy for me and my new circumstances, for it is what I truly want, indeed what we both want most ardently.

Lord Henri-Antoine Hesham has asked me to be his wife, and I have accepted, and we are to be married at the end of the week.

We are in love and while this was a speedy courtship, His Lordship's family are reconciled to the match, for which I am most humbly grateful. It makes us both happy that Lord Henri-Antoine's family, most particularly his mother, Her Grace the Duchess—who is the kindest, most loving mother-in-law a girl could wish for—and his brother and sister-in-law, Their Graces the Duke and Duchess, have welcomed me with open arms and open hearts.

I also write to inform you that His Lordship has written to Uncle de Crespigny, who is my legal guardian, as a matter of procedure, to ask for his consent to our union. Accompanying his letter is one from his brother the Duke. Both letters were sent by liveried courier, with the servant to await an immediate written response of affirmation from my uncle so that plans for the wedding can continue apace. Dr. Moore, the Archbishop of Canterbury, has already inked our Special License, so the marriage has the blessing of the Church. Thus, the consent from my uncle, so I am assured by my future husband and my future brother-in-law, is a mere formality, and one we all believe will be readily and eagerly accepted.

The wedding is to be a small, intimate affair of immediate family only, and to be held in the Roxton family chapel. My dearest friend, for whom I was bridesmaid, and who is now Lady Cavendish, is to stand as my attendant, and her new husband Sir

John, who is His Lordship's best friend, will stand as his best man. It has all worked out rather well and to our mutual satisfaction. I know you will not mind in the least that I issued no invitations of my own, for how could you leave your important work, my dear Dr. Warner, to travel all this way to attend what is a very small occasion. And as my aunt and uncle are just returned from Paris, I suspect they too have had enough of travel for the time being. And there is the small fact that there is truly no time for anyone to ready themselves for such an event at such short notice.

I intend to write to my aunt and uncle apprising them of my news, though it is a formality only, as it will come after His Lordship's request for consent. At least my letter will not be such a shock to them, as this must be for you.

I do hope that in time you will be reconciled to the startling change in my circumstances, and I assure you both that I fell in love with and am marrying a most loving, kind, and generous man, who also happens to be the son of a duke, and the brother of another. Being wife to a man who is possessed of a good and honorable character will be my great honor. My elevation in society to be at his side as Her Ladyship will, I assure you, not change my character in the least.

I hope you will allow me to pay my respects once we come up to town at the end of September and are settled at our Park Street address.

Please give baby George a kiss from me. I shall miss my visits to the nursery.

I look forward to being in your company again in the not too distant future.

Your devoted cousin,

Lisa

Soon to be known by her married name of Lady Henri-Antoine

Hesham

LORD HENRI-ANTOINE HESHAM, DIARY ENTRY

[*Translated from the French.*]

July 11, 1786

Dearest Papa, tomorrow I marry the woman to whom I have given my heart and my soul. I have never felt so full of happiness, and optimism for the future, and those feelings are all because of her. Lisa loves me unreservedly, and has told me so many times. Not that I need her reassurance, because I believe her. But she does love to tell me and I love to hear her say it. Her love has lifted a weight that has been pressing on my heart for too long, since you left us, in fact. For although I will always have Maman's unconditional love, it was to you I turned most for support, and it was you who understood me best. Without you I have been adrift in that sea you spoke about, and for far too long. But now, with Lisa, I have found a safe harbor, one in which I can truly be myself; it is one where I wish to remain and never leave.

You knew, and told me so, how I would feel in every particular when I fell in love, because that is what you felt for Maman when you fell in love and married her. And as a boy, I would wonder how it was my parents could spend their time together without saying a word to each other, and yet look so happy and content. While I lay on the chaise longue recovering, I would watch you at your desk, and Maman in her favorite chair, or beside me on the chaise longue. You would occasionally look up from your work and at Maman while she was reading, or when she read aloud to me, and I would watch your mouth curve of its own accord into a smile you bestowed upon her alone. I did wonder if you were even aware you were doing it. I do not think you ever knew I was watching you. Perhaps you did, and did not care. At the time, I frowningly wondered what it was she had just read or said to amuse you. But it was not amusement at all, was it, but the smile that accompanies a feeling of utter contentment and love, that here is the woman you love beyond reason, and who loves you in the same way, and you are together and you cannot quite believe it. I now find myself having the exact same thoughts and reaction when I am with Lisa. It matters not if we are in a large family gathering or alone, just the two of us. And she will, like Maman did with you, return my smile knowingly, often the smile is just in her eyes, but I see it and my heart gives the oddest little leap and my throat dries with emotion, knowing that she truly loves me, and that she knows I love her, and yet not one word have we exchanged. Is it not the most marvelous feeling?

We will visit you tomorrow, after the wedding breakfast. Lisa wishes to lay her bouquet at your feet, and I shall tell you all about our intended bridal trip, for I am taking her abroad. *Bonsoir, mon cher père.*

ANTONIA, DUCHESS OF KINROSS, DIARY ENTRY

[*Translated from the French.*]

July 12, 1786

Renard, today our little boy was married. I am so very happy for him, and for them! I know you would be just as happy, and so very, very proud of your son.

The wedding was a small family affair held in the chapel. Henri-Antoine looked very handsome and somber. He was possibly as nervous as you were on our wedding day. Though I do not think any groom was ever as nervous as you were on our day! Naturally Lisa made a beautiful bride, and when Henri-Antoine saw her he relaxed enough to smile. Renard, I tell you, I have never seen our son smile so much and for a whole day! He could not have wiped the smile from his face had he tried. But I do not think he wanted to. He is so happy. They are so happy. Their happiness brought tears to my eyes, and not only to mine.

Jack and Teddy delayed their honeymoon so that Jack could stand as Henri-Antoine's best man, and Teddy could be Lisa's attendant (as Lisa had been hers just over a week ago). Two best friends have married two best friends, and it could not have turned out any better had it been contrived! All four young people are overjoyed at this outcome, and I predict both couples will enjoy a lifetime of unparalleled closeness. Everyone in the family is delighted about this, too.

Jonathon gave Lisa away, and was honored to be asked by her. He proudly strutted up the aisle with her on his arm as if she were indeed his own daughter. Elsie was excited to be Lisa's flower girl, and clung to her side for most of the wedding breakfast, which was delightful. Julian and Deb and all the children, Mary and Christopher with their three little ones, Cousin Charles, who was honored to be one of Henri-Antoine's attendants and so delayed his return to France, and Kate Paget were all in attendance. And of course, the senior members of Henri-Antoine's household were turned out in their Sunday best. Michel Gallet had the distinction of standing alongside Jack, Charles, and Frederick, your grandson looking very proper and proud to be so favored by his uncle.

The eight lads in their livery formed an honor guard, and when the newly-married couple passed between them as they left the chapel, these hulks of men gave three rousing cheers. This came as a complete surprise to Henri-Antoine and Lisa, who were startled and then fell on each other laughing before turning and applauding the lads, who in turn bowed to them with great courteousness. This had everyone smiling and the children cheering in response. We all sat down to a breakfast in the family dining room, with Julian giving a speech warmly welcoming Lisa into the family, which his brother greatly appreciated.

Tomorrow Jack and Teddy are off to Bath to begin their honeymoon, while Henri-Antoine and Lisa will remain here at Treat for a few weeks while they plan their bridal trip. They are going abroad and want to travel as far as Constantinople. Henri-Antoine hopes to stay in the house we had there all those years ago when he was a little boy. They will make visits along the way there to various medical facilities and consult with physicians for the work of the Fournier Foundation.

They also hope to procure medicinals from the Ottoman physicians to help alleviate Henri-Antoine's symptoms, if not his seizures. Do you remember that when we consulted with these learned men they advised, given he was just a little boy at the time, waiting until he was older and we could be certain the seizures they could not be cured, before giving him what they prescribed for sufferers of the falling sickness.

As much as I will miss them, such a trip will be a wonderful time for them both, and provide them with a lifetime of memories.

And because of their mutual interest in the advancement of medical science, as a wedding gift Henri-Antoine has made Lisa patroness of his foundation. Lord and Lady Henri-Antoine Hesham will be joint patrons and head the Fournier Foundation's board of trustees, she to have equal standing with him in all decisions regarding the foundation's operation and distribution of its funding. This he has had written up in a contract of sorts, and means to write and inform the other trustees of how the foundation is to go on from here, now he is married, and his wife is to share in all his endeavors. Lisa is thrilled with this gift. It is as if our son has showered her in diamonds and pearls, and presented her with her own chateau. Of course, all of these things he can do, too, but she sees this partnership as the most precious gift he could have bestowed upon her, and I love her all the more for it. It makes them both very happy to have this shared passion, and interests. Did I not tell you they are perfect for each other?

I will bring Germanicus and Livia with me to visit you tomorrow, for I do not think you have seen either since Livia was whelped. *Jusqu'à demain, mon amour.* A xo

LADY HENRI-ANTOINE HESHAM TO MRS. HAROLD HUMPHREYS

Lady Henri-Antoine Hesham, Treat via Alston, Hampshire, to Mrs. Harold Humphreys, Humphreys Haberdashery, crn. Gerrard and Princes Street, Soho, London.

August 1, 1786

Dear Mrs. Humphreys,

I write to offer your niece Betsy Bannister a position within my household as wardrobe mistress and head seamstress. She will receive a handsome monthly remuneration, an annual clothing allowance, and have her own room. And while she will be in charge of my clothes and closet, and supervise a junior seamstress, she will come under the direction of my personal lady's maid. That position has yet to be filled, but soon will be, and by a suitably qualified and experienced woman. Interviews are expected to be conducted early next week. Should Betsy arrive before the position of lady's maid is decided, she will be supervised by the household's major domo M'sieur Gallet.

The position I offer Betsy is one that will require her, like all our upper servants, to travel between our townhouse in Park Street, Westminster, the apartment at Treat here in Hampshire, and His Lordship's estate near Bath. As you can appreciate, all three residences have wardrobes to maintain, and clothing and other accoutrements that will require transportation to and from each residence. These must be accounted for as well as cared for, and will come under Betsy's custody.

The most challenging aspect of the position may be at the very start of her tenure because His Lordship is taking me on a bridal trip to Constantinople. I will want Betsy to be part of our entourage. We will be abroad for approximately nine months to a year. While away she, like all our servants, which will approximately number between twenty to thirty individuals, will come under the jurisdiction of His Lordship's major domo.

I realize this is a lot for you and Betsy to take in, and that it is very short notice. Indeed I would like your response and Betsy's answer within the week so M'sieur Gallet can finalize our travel arrangements. And if Betsy does take up this offer, and I sincerely hope she will, I am aware that you will suffer the loss of her, and her assistance in the shop and with the various clients Betsy visits in their homes. I am thus prepared to offer you compensation for the absence of your niece, and pay you in one lump sum and at once, half a year of Betsy's salary so that you will have the means to find a replacement as soon as possible.

I assure you that if at any time Betsy decides she cannot be away from London and you, and she pines for England, she will be sent home at our expense, for I do not want her unhappy. I will of course provide her with a reference of service. You will not be required to reimburse me any of the monies paid to you in lieu should Betsy wish to return home.

Would you please discuss all of this with Betsy and reply at your earliest convenience. Payment of a courier to expedite a reply will be met by His Lordship upon receipt. When I have Betsy's answer, and if it is in the affirmative, I will make arrangements to have you paid the compensation at once, and His Lordship's carriage will fetch Betsy and whatever belongings she chooses to bring with her.

I do hope you will both see this as an opportunity worth taking.

Sincerely,
Lady Henri-Antoine Hesham

LADY HENRI-ANTOINE HESHAM TO ANTONIA, DUCHESS OF KINROSS

Lady Henri-Antoine Hesham, the White House on Third Hill, Constantinople, to Her Grace the Most Noble Duchess of Kinross, Leven Castle via Kinross, Fife, Scotland.

[*Translated from the French.*]

The White House on Third Hill, Constantinople,
August 12, 1787

Dear Maman-Duchess,

I trust this letter finds you, Papa-Kinross, and Elsie in the best of good health.

Before I write anything else, I, we, thank you from the bottom of our hearts for the truly special and touching gift you sent to help us celebrate the first anniversary of our marriage. I can hardly believe it is thirteen months to the day since my life changed forever. The months have gone by too quickly, but each one has been more magical than the last, and you know from our letters how very happy we are.

Your gift arrived only two days ago, so it was indeed a wonderful surprise! Neither of us had any expectations of what it could be, though Henri-Antoine knew immediately he removed the wooden box from its crate and shed its wrappings. He set the box on the low table before us, and it was well we were seated on cushions and just inches from the ground because he swayed and grabbed the table edge. You can imagine I thought he was unwell, but he assured me he was not. Before he opened the lid, he gently ran his fingers over the box's polished surface in the same manner I have seen him do when calming a frightened dog or petting a cat, as if the object had life and was a treasured pet. And when he slowly opened it out to reveal the inlaid interior and the playing pieces and cups within, there were tears in his eyes. He was so overcome that I remained silent, yet could hardly wait for him to tell me the significance of this playing box, and most particularly its special significance for him.

When he told me that this was the very backgammon board you and his father played on every day of your married life, I, too, was overcome, and remained speechless. He told me in a shaking voice how he would watch you both from the chaise longue, and how he often felt an intruder because when you played at backgammon you forgot everyone else and it was as if it was just the two of you in the library. But he also told me that it was you who taught him how to play. And he recalled the day he won his first game from his father, and his father's look of incredulity that his eight-year-old son had beaten him at his own game. That memory had Henri-Antoine grinning. Though he then was incredulous himself that you had parted with this most treasured and loved item.

But I understand why you did, and you know, do you not, Maman-Duchess, that we will cherish this as you do, and always will. Henri-Antoine has already written to thank you, and no doubt he told you I am a complete novice at the game. Though I am certain you knew this was so. We have decided that we will honor your gift by playing each evening, while having our Turkish coffee. I am very willing to learn, and Henri-Antoine is already proving a patient if exacting teacher. I have a plan to improve my game so that he will be more than a little surprised (and no doubt think it all down to his superior teaching skills). When he visits the coffee houses (which you know are denied to women) to smoke a hookah and play at backgammon with the local men, I intend to practice my game with Michel, who Henri-Antoine let slip is more than a tolerable opponent. In this way I hope to emulate his feat as an eight-year-old, and beat him at his own game—one day!

Please thank Elsie for her recent letter enclosing her delightful watercolors of her dear little kitten Blanche, and of the loch, and the pretty purple flowers. I have placed these and her letters in a specially-bound book which I keep in my boudoir and will show her when we return home. I will write to her separately of course, but direct that letter to Crecy, so she will have that waiting for her when you arrive there at the end of the month.

Do you recall how in my previous letter I was on a mission to find a suitable companion for her dolls? Well I have finally found her! Mlle Yvette and Signorina Simonetta are to have a new friend. I have named her Sevil, which means 'to be loved' in Turkish. And I know she will be. Sevil is the same size as Elsie's other companions, and has ivory skin, dark hair, dark eyes, and a rosebud mouth. She is dressed in the costume of a female of the sultan's harem in pantaloons, long over-jacket, and has a turban atop her hair, all in vibrant silks. Her hair is free flowing and so thick it can be arranged in all manner of styles. I have asked Betsy to fashion Sevil half a dozen similar outfits in different silks, and also to make her several pairs of matching slippers. We found tiny silver bracelets for her wrists and ankles at the markets. And I commissioned one of the woodworkers to make her a special box for her to lie in, lined in velvet, and a small clothespress for her clothing and various accessories. She also has a most wondrous miniature stringed instrument called a Tambur (we have an adult-sized one to present to Jack) which can be tuned and played if one is dexterous enough to pluck delicately at the strings. I cannot wait for Elsie and her companions to meet Sevil. Henri-Antoine says, and he is quite right, that I am as excited as if the doll were mine, for I have indeed derived great pleasure in having Sevil dressed, and in commissioning the making of her accessories.

I had crated and shipped the second lot of silks and threads you requested, and Henri-Antoine has visited the carpet warehouse twice to see progress for himself. As the order is such a large one, he is greeted by the weavers as if their sultan has come amongst them, and as you can imagine he does not disappoint, and plays his part, as do the lads. I found a Turkish coffee service and all its pieces like the one Henri-Antoine remembers you using and he drinking from the little cups when you stayed here. He says it is similar to the travel set His Grace has at Treat. I am hopeful it will please you and Papa-Kinross. I liked it so much I bought four complete sets: One for you, one for Jack and Teddy, one for the townhouse in Park Street, and one for the house in Bath. Henri-Antoine intends to fashion a room in both houses in the Ottoman style, and has ordered what amounts to two entire rooms worth of what is necessary to replicate our private sitting room here, everything from the silk cushions, hangings, wallpapers, carpets (you see why the weavers venerate him!), low stools, couches, and even two nargiles. I am told a nargile is the same thing with a different name as the hookah Papa-Kinross brought with him from the subcontinent. Henri-Antoine insists Papa-Kinross have one for use at Leven.

My dear husband tells me he was introduced to the pleasures of smoking from the water-pipe by His Grace in his teens, though perhaps that was not something he wished you to discover, so please do not take Papa-Kinross to task, Maman-Duchess. But such expertise as Henri-Antoine has in using a water-pipe has come in useful here. The physicians we have consulted with have provided him with a special herbal tobacco, a substitute for the usual tobacco used in the water-pipe, which they assure us will help alleviate his symptoms, if not stop the onset of a seizure.

On that score, he had a most severe attack two weeks ago, which I believe was brought on by the lack of proper recuperation from a seizure the previous week. And it is all because he insisted on accompanying me to the textile markets during the heat of the day. I had arranged for my lady's maid Niven and Betsy to go with me, and as you know I never step out of our compound without two of the lads as our escort. I have gone alone in this manner to the markets on several occasions, but Henri-Antoine was determined and intractable that this time he would come with me. I knew his stubbornness was not only because he was still feeling unwell, but because it had become a point of male pride for him to be my escort. This was because Sir Jonas Wetherby (I told you about the scholar of Oriental languages attached to the embassy in a previous letter), dared to make an unguarded remark under the influence of too much spirits to Henri-Antoine at the Occidental Club, and before others. Sir Jonas dared to suggest that His Lordship was cavalier in allowing such a beauty (me) to roam about Constantinople's streets without her husband's protection. That while I had my lady's maid and liveried servants with me, they were no substitute for a young bride having her husband's arm. That a husband was the best and only signal to the locals that here is a female who is not only carefully nurtured, and of the highest possible rank within her own society, but she is to be treated with the utmost respect, and not to be trifled with by the local men.

I do not know what angered Henri-Antoine the most: To be lectured to about his want of manners as a gentleman, his seeming neglect as a husband, or that Sir Jonas would have the impertinence to suggest the locals would ever dare 'trifle' with His Lordship's wife. All of these, is my guess. No matter that Sir Jonas is quite a stupid man, for all his abilities as a translator. He may be good at his job, but he must lack basic comprehension skills, for anyone with a modicum of understanding would not make such an unguarded remark to a social superior, and never to a new husband, and most definitely not to His Lordship.

I have no idea what Henri-Antoine said by way of reply, only that the sting in Sir Jonas's words led to him getting out of bed well before he should have. A day spent enjoying the cool waters of our plunge pool and the use of the nargile would have served him better. But I realized there was no use offering up this suggestion when his male pride had taken a battering. And so he came with me. To shorten a sorry story, this second attack was most severe and required that the lads spirit him away down a darkened alley, and there we remained until the attack subsided, and his sedan chair could be fetched to carry him home. He was put back to bed where he remained for four days.

It is the worst attack since our stay in Padua. And while I am all sympathy for his suffering I did tell him it served him to rights for not staying abed until he was fully recovered. I also stated that I refuse to leave our compound again under any circumstance, barring invasion by the Russians, if he could not offer me the assurance he would rest until he was well. And if he did not understand me then perhaps I should call in Sir Jonas to translate my words into a language he not only understood, but which was simple enough for him to comprehend. My dear husband informed me he had already ordered the servants to bar Sir Jonas from admittance to our house, so he would not have to suffer that fool again. He grumbled some more but soon apologized. His accompanying look of affected contrition (though I believe he was truly sorry) was such that I burst into giggles. This had him grinning in response, and all was forgiven, though he refused to forgive Sir Jonas. Which I said was reasonable, and we kissed and made up. Maman-Duchess this is the only disagreement we have had in our first year of marriage.

As to possible invasion by the Russians, I know the situation in the Crimea has been reported in the English newssheets, and you must be worried lest this war between the Turks and the Russians arrives here in Constantinople. Henri-Antoine says the coffee houses are full of nothing else but talk of war, that it will be soon, for the Sultan cannot allow Catherine to take what does not belong to her. This state of affairs, with the threat of war imminent and all that entails for a nation facing invasion, means we have already made arrangements to leave here and return home as soon as possible. All our belongings that are not absolutely necessary for our day-to-day existence have been crated, and these with the sedan chairs and carriages are already at the docks ready to be loaded aboard ship. We leave in a week's time, under sail, so that we return to England with all speed. It is not only the coming of war that motivates us but because we have been away long enough now, and because of Teddy's most wonderful and longed-for news!

We are both so thrilled and excited that Teddy and Jack are finally to become parents. We have been expecting this for some months now, and dared not to hope against hope it would be sooner rather than later. I know Teddy was grateful not to fall pregnant almost at once, but with the passing of months, a hint of apprehension had crept into her letters that she had not already done so. And just as I received her letter expressing this apprehension another arrived almost the very next day with news of her pregnancy and the baby due in the new year, around the time of her baby sister's second birthday, which would be a lovely double celebration for both families. We are so looking forward to being home for the birth, and to take on the role of doting godparents.

Which brings me to answer the question you asked in the letter previous to the one you just sent, about my health. Naturally Henri-Antoine is fully apprised, but you are the only other to whom I will confide. Perhaps one day I may tell Teddy, but at the present time she must focus on her own health and her baby.

I did allow myself to submit to a physical examination, and by one of the most learned and respected midwives in this city. She has delivered more babies than any male physician here. My interpreter assured me that even the women of the Sultan's harem trust her with their lives, and with their fertility. I would never have permitted a male, no matter how learned, to examine me in this most intimate of ways, but I felt exceedingly comfortable in her presence and with her manner. And while I know Henri-Antoine is not at all bothered at the prospect of us remaining childless, and says so with such confidence that I believe him, he also says, and I know you will take this in the right manner, that my barren state is a blessing in disguise, because he has no wish to bring a child into the world who suffers his affliction. And I would be lying to you if I said I did not agree with him. Yet there are times, not very often, when I allow my reasoning to scatter and I daydream of possibilities. So with this in mind, and to have peace of mind, I permitted the midwife to examine me.

The outcome was not as I expected. The examination itself was more discomforting to my dignity than anything else, and when she had finished she was smiling, so I took that as a good sign. Through the interpreter she told me I was indeed female, which made me wonder if something was lost in the translation because how could I be anything else, until it was explained to me (and perhaps you are aware of this, but I most certainly was not) that there are women in this world—and this shocked me, though I do not disbelieve her—who may have every outward appearance of being a female, but who are devoid of the reproductive organs necessary to conceive and bear children. I would be lying if I told you this did not greatly unsettle me. Yet, after the examination she was able to assure me that I am indeed in possession of a womb. So in theory at least, I can grow a child within me. But she did add that my womb is small for a female my age and even for one who has never had children. She said this may account for my lack of menses. And it is her learned opinion that for me conception may just be a matter of time. She said as I am young I have many years, indeed decades, of hope left to me.

To be frank, Maman-Duchess, we do not want to spend decades in hope, and so we will put this new-found knowledge aside and return to living our lives. I mean to live each day as I have every other day since my marriage, and that is as a loving wife, companion, and helpmate to your son, whom you know, as surely as the sun rises every morning, I love with every fiber of my being. And we shall concentrate on the great task we have ahead of us in making the Fournier Foundation not only our legacy, but Monseigneur's and the family's legacy, too.

This will make you chuckle. The midwife prescribed me a herbal medicinal concoction which she says is an aid to fertility. I have no notion if it will be beneficial in the way it is intended or not, but Henri-Antoine insists I at least try it. Secretly, I think he is pleased to not be the only one taking concoctions that taste foul, and which with the best of intentions we tell him to endure for his health. So we take our medicine like good children, together, both resisting the urge to pull a face, not wanting to be the first to give in, and doing our best to appear unaffected by the foul taste. Neither of us wants to be the first to grab for the tumbler of punch within reach to wash out our mouths. So we make the effort not to look at each other while taking our medicine, particularly when the servants are with us. But if we are alone and we dare to glance up and our eyes meet, we lose all sense of decorum and burst into giggles, and sometimes so hard we momentarily stop breathing. We fall about on the cushions, eyes watering. One time a servant entered while we were in this silly state and thought we had both been poisoned, threw the tray in the air and ran out of the room screaming. This only made us laugh harder, particularly when Michel dared to glare at us with a mixture of exasperation and delight, like a parent wishing to scold his children but unable to do so because they are enjoying themselves too much. For his benefit and to save his sanity, we came to our senses and tried our best to appear contrite, though the tears of laughter were still running down our cheeks.

Have you ever seen Henri-Antoine giggling so hard he must hold his sides? It is a joy to behold and a privilege, for you know how stern he is with himself and how in control when he is under the public eye. Did his father ever giggle when alone with you, I wonder? You of course do not have to answer me, Maman-Duchess, for I think he must have at least chuckled and perhaps laughed hard enough in your company to bring tears to his eyes. I thought you would like to know this about your son.

I must away to supper. We are having it on the rooftop, now the sun has set. And because it is so hot, we will take a midnight swim in the plunge pool, and there float and look up at the twinkling night sky. Our time away and our stay here have been magical, but we are both eager to return home, to you, and to our family, to begin this next chapter of our lives, together.

With love,
Lisa
Lady Henri-Antoine Hesham
I write my married name with such wonder, pride, and joy.
xo

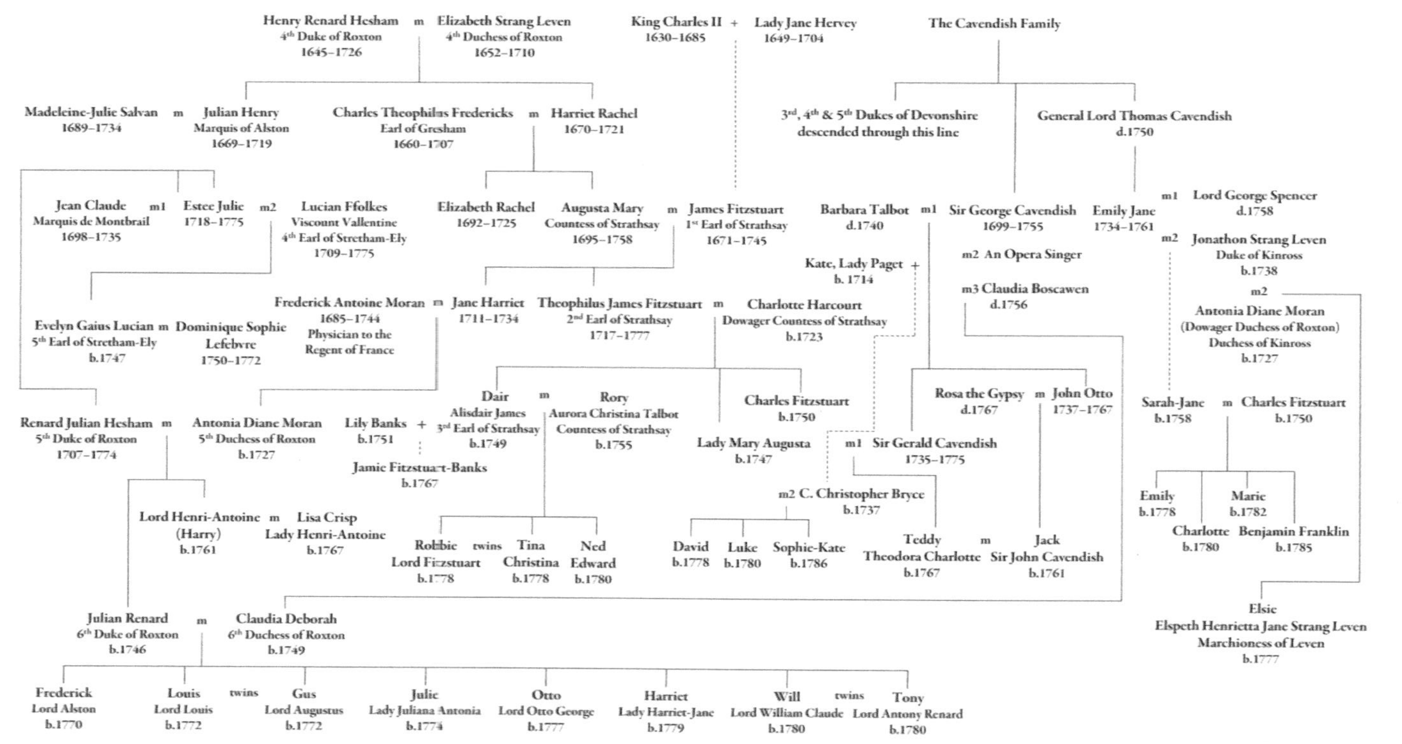

Henry Renard Hesham m Elizabeth Strang Leven
4th Duke of Roxton   4th Duchess of Roxton
1645–1726   1652–1710
King Charles II + Lady Jane Hervey
1630–1685   1649–1704
The Cavendish Family
Madeleine-Julie Salvan m Julian Henry
1689–1734   Marquis of Alston
                           1669–1719
Charles Theophilus Fredericks m Harriet Rachel
Earl of Gresham   1670–1721
1660–1707
3rd, 4th & 5th Dukes of Devonshire
descended through this line
General Lord Thomas Cavendish
d.1750
Jean Claude m1 Estee Julie m2 Lucian Ffolkes
Marquis de Montbrail 1718–1775   Viscount Vallentine
1698–1735   4th Earl of Stretham-Ely
                                  1709–1775
Elizabeth Rachel Augusta Mary m James Fitzstuart
1692–1725   Countess of Strathsay 1st Earl of Strathsay
                  1695–1758   1671–1745
Barbara Talbot m1 Sir George Cavendish Emily Jane
d.1740   1699–1755   1734–1761
m1 Lord George Spencer
    d.1758
m2 Jonathon Strang Leven
    Duke of Kinross
    b.1738
Kate, Lady Paget +
b.1714
m2 An Opera Singer
m3 Claudia Boscawen
    d.1756
m2
Antonia Diane Moran
(Dowager Duchess of Roxton)
Duchess of Kinross
b.1727
Evelyn Gaius Lucian m Dominique Sophie
5th Earl of Stretham-Ely Lefebvre
b.1747   1750–1772
Frederick Antoine Moran m Jane Harriet
1685–1744   1711–1734
Physician to the
Regent of France
Theophilus James Fitzstuart m Charlotte Harcourt
2nd Earl of Strathsay   Dowager Countess of Strathsay
1717–1777   b.1723
Rosa the Gypsy m John Otto
d.1767   1737–1767
Sarah-Jane m Charles Fitzstuart
b.1758   b.1750
Renard Julian Hesham m Antonia Diane Moran Lily Banks +
5th Duke of Roxton   5th Duchess of Roxton b.1751
1707–1774   b.1727
Dair m Rory
Alisdair James Aurora Christina Talbot
3rd Earl of Strathsay Countess of Strathsay
b.1749   b.1755
Charles Fitzstuart
b.1750
m1 Sir Gerald Cavendish
    1735–1775
Jamie Fitzstuart-Banks
b.1767
Lady Mary Augusta
b.1747
Emily Marie
b.1778 b.1782
Lord Henri-Antoine m Lisa Crisp
(Harry)   Lady Henri-Antoine
b.1761   b.1767
Robbie twins Tina Ned
Lord Fitzstuart Christina Edward
b.1778   b.1778   b.1780
David Luke Sophie-Kate
b.1778 b.1780 b.1786
m2 C. Christopher Bryce
b.1737
Teddy m Jack
Theodora Charlotte Sir John Cavendish
b.1767   b.1761
Charlotte Benjamin Franklin
b.1780   b.1785
Julian Renard m Claudia Deborah
6th Duke of Roxton 6th Duchess of Roxton
b.1746   b.1749
Elsie
Elspeth Henrietta Jane Strang Leven
Marchioness of Leven
b.1777
Frederick Louis twins Gus Julie Otto Harriet Will twins Tony
Lord Alston Lord Louis Lord Augustus Lady Juliana Antonia Lord Otto George Lady Harriet-Jane Lord William Claude Lord Antony Renard
b.1770 b.1772 b.1772 b.1774 b.1777 b.1779 b.1780 b.1780

BEHIND-THE-SCENES

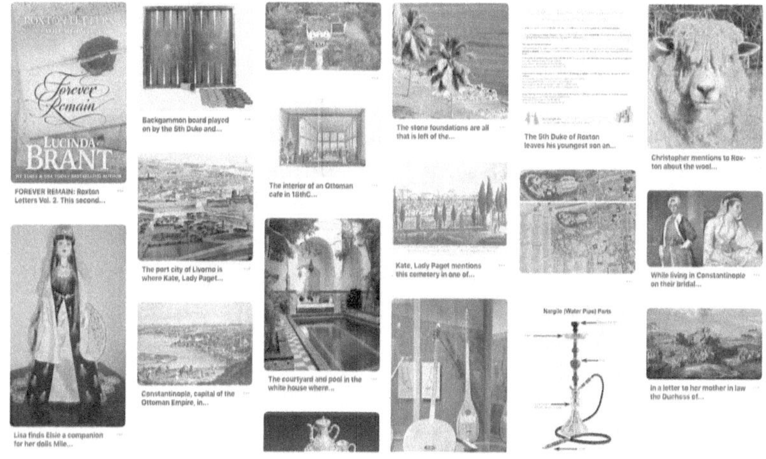

Explore the places, objects, and history in
Forever Remain on Pinterest.

www.pinterest.com/lucindabrant